Lines..d

by

Roger Barnes

Thanks are owed to transport artist Malcolm Root
for allowing us to reproduce his magnificent oil painting
of an East Anglian branch line and use it in our cover design.
This and other such pictures appear in:
'Malcolm Root's Railway Paintings'
published by Halsgrove: ISBN 1 84114 366 9

Linesend
A tale of a Suffolk railway
ISBN: 978-0-9564855-1-9

Published by **Pawprint Publishin**g
14, Polstead Close, Stowmarket, Suffolk IP14 2PJ

in memory of Gerry Fiennes
Who would know that not a word
could possibly be true

and Brian Leighton
Who would know that some of it could be!

Ceremony

The signal went down; a whistle blew, putting up an unwatchful thrush much to the relief of the bird and the consternation of the porter's ginger Tom which had spent some twenty minutes stalking it. Just to show its spite it viciously savaged the vicar's wife instead, immediately prior to treating the local police Alsatian to a glare which guaranteed its early retirement. The moth-eaten green flag was shown, and Gilbert Shenge, station-master of Slowmeadow station, had given the 'right away' to his last train.

As he turned, the boys of the local Boys Brigade band finished a performance of their highly original version of 'Blaze Away,' its abject tunelessness exacerbated by the fact that the bandleader, one Ramsbottom Simple, having insisted on conducting from the steps of the guard's van, had consequently departed with the train.

There followed an uneasy silence during which Sir George noticed that if the light was right, and that snivelling police dog-handler moved his head somewhat to the left, he could see right through Sybil Craxton's dress. He wished he'd noticed this odd phenomenon sooner.

"Trick of the light," he thought.

His train of thought was however soon to be disturbed by the voice of John Sleet-Ashe, General Manager of the East South-Eastern Region of the newly formed British Railways.

"Come on Sir George, get on with it: the 'Flax Weaver and Pheasant's' got a market licence today, and if we get a move on here, we can be there by three."

Sir George, past chairman of the Mid-East South-Eastern Light Railway Company Limited - very limited, many thought - stood up, or rather lurched to his feet. Six pink gins and a bottle of Piesporter '48 at lunch in the 'Maiden's Delight' had had three effects on the gallant knight: he almost at once noticed that the platform of Slowmeadow station seemed to him to be in need of urgent underpinning, especially if it were to be capable of supporting his weight for the duration of his speech. He noticed that he felt an equally urgent need to break wind, probably from both ends though he was by no means certain about this; and that his voice was slurred. The latter effect he decided to disregard since he was fully aware that his voice was permanently slurred: he put that down to an excess of chlorine in the local tap water, not that he ever drank much of that.

Sir George shuffled his papers with a deliberate care in order to render anything he might have prepared, though equally deliberately hadn't, totally meaningless. Sir George always took great pride in his personal sense of occasion and had decided that this wasn't one!

He stared at the gathered crowd, or rather he stared in the direction he supposed the crowd to be, and coughed loudly. The cough was almost a mistake, for at that precise moment Sir George became aware that the wine had had a fourth effect!

"This railway was opened in 1900..."

“1901,” muttered Sleet-Ashe.

“It was late even then,” whispered Sybil Craxton to Harry Trumps, the station’s totally deaf porter-cum-booking-clerk. Harry nodded knowingly and noticed for the first time that Sir George’s flies were undone. Sybil Craxton noticed with some regret but not a little relief that his long-johns were not.

“…And we are gathered here my lords, ladies and gentlemen…” He had been reminded of the latter two social classifications of gender by his increasingly uncomfortable personal needs and the large signs on the opposite platform, “...to bid a fond farewell to the Company’s longest serving employee, Gilbert Shenge. Er Shenge...”, and here Sir George re-emphasised the surname of the humble railway servant who occupied the dais with him, evidently remembering their different social positions and having suddenly become rather afraid that familiarity, in the continued use of Shenge’s Christian name, might breed contempt. In this he need not have worried, for in common with most people, irrespective of social position, Gilbert Shenge held Sir George in the utmost contempt anyway. Still for good measure, Sir George repeated his surname once more.
“Shenge joined the railway on the day it was opened, fifty-one years ago today…”

“Fifty years, you fool,” muttered Sleet- Ashe in despair, beginning to think that before very long he would have to get the inscription changed on the cheap presentation watch; seven and six from ‘Headquarters and General Supply,’ complete with receipt for five pounds.

“…And retires today, fifty-one years later…” added Sir George deliberately and completely ignoring the General Manager’s comment, “as stationmaster of all five of the line’s stations, having served the railway, I might add, for over fifty years.”

Ignoring the incorrect starting date - Sir George was sure his arithmetic was impeccable - he watched Sybil Craxton nonchalantly flick her riding crop against her dress-covered shapely thigh. He mused it was not for nothing that he had been beaten regularly at school: he thought briefly of matron, paused, smiled a distant smile and continued.

"We are most pleased to present you, er Hubert…"

"Gilbert, you dunderhead," forced Sleet-Ashe under his exasperated breath.

"...With this beautifully engraved gold watch. You'll be able to keep the times of all the trains on the line as they pass by the window of that cottage of yours, eh what?"

Shenge had already considered that this was probably the last thing he would do with it; even if he bothered to take the wretched thing home at all!

"Don't forget the British Railways pension," groaned Sleet-Ashe.

"What?" questioned Sir George.

"The pension, you old duffer, Shenge's pension."

"And I must offer you an exceedingly generous Company pension of one pound seventeen shillings and five-pence per week... for life."

Sir George added the last two words, after what he considered to be a suitable pause, for the benefit of the crowd. His use of the word 'company' earlier in the sentence, had, he had hoped, served to create the illusion that the pension was in some odd way his own personal gift, as ex-chairman of the Railway, and not the stationmaster's right as a retiring employee of a recently-nationalised industry. Sir George waited for the applause of an appreciative crowd. There was none!

Sir George nodded at Shenge with a movement of the head so imperceptible that the latter could easily have been left uncertain as to its meaning.

Gilbert Shenge stepped forward; this was, he mistakenly thought, his moment. He held out his hand in order to receive his watch and perhaps even to shake the hand of his senile, drunkard ex-employer. Unfortunately his thought was wrong. It was Sir George's moment, as he had always intended that it should be. Brilliantly upstaging Shenge, Sir George continued.

"But before I make the presentation I must first say a few words about the Mid-East South-Eastern Light Railway…"

"A very few words I hope," thought Sleet-Ashe looking anxiously at his watch and noticing not for the first time a dryness at the back of his throat.

Sleet-Ashe need not have worried. At the back of the platform there was a slight commotion as Lt. Col. Putney Dandridge, late of the Indian Army and late practically everywhere else, fainted. With a military precision that had been singularly lacking throughout the old soldier's long career, the elderly warrior had timed his swoon to coincide perfectly with the word 'railway.' So perfect was its timing that it might almost have been rehearsed!

Sir George dropped his bunch of blank papers instantly and broke wind, confident in the knowledge that the breeze would carry away both the papers and any odour, whilst the buzz of excitement from the gathering would cover the sound of his long contained yet much enjoyed raucous fart. He rushed or rather shuffled forward with a contrived yet convincing look of concern upon his red face.

"I say Dandridge, are you all right?"

Dandridge groaned in a reasonably convincing way and then fell silent. If Sir George had not known the old soldier better or had been just a little more sober himself then he might have been worried, but since he drank to prevent worry and never worried when he was drunk, he remained totally unconcerned.

"Look I'd better get the poor old chap in the Rover and cart him off to Muttering Market. I expect it's his old war wound playing him up again. Gives him a lot of trouble in the hotter weather, don't you know?"

It had crossed Sleet-Ashe's mind that the problem was more likely to be a peptic ulcer from too much gin and tonic. Sleet-Ashe had as usual completely misjudged the true significance of the situation.

"Oh! Here you are Osbert or whatever your damned name is: take your bloody watch and be quick about it. There's no time to lose. They'll pay your pension at the post office I expect. Now out of the way there's a good chap. Ashe, Ashe, damn you, are you coming? Help me get the old fool into the car..."

Feet dragged, tongues buzzed, doors slammed and an engine was started with some considerable difficulty, filling the air with a cloud of strange smelling smoke not unlike that which you get from the wick of a hurricane lamp which has been turned up too high. Sir George's battered Rover 14 leaped or rather bucked out of the gates of Slowmeadow station-yard and backfired loudly causing Sybil Craxton's horse to bolt in terror.

Twenty yards down the road, just around the first bend and consequently out of sight of the milling crowd the Colonel made what can only be described as a most remarkable recovery. His first words as he opened his eyes being...

“If you’re making for the ‘Flax Weaver and Pheasant’ it’s second left and third right.”

Back at the station, the crowd on the little platform was clearing unbelievably quickly. Everyone, including Gilbert Shenge, was rushing into the lane in order to watch the lovely Sybil Craxton chasing her horse. There was a good chance that her dress would be blown up by the breeze some thought, or better still, thought Harry Trumps, be caught on a briar and ripped completely off. And thus it was that whenever the lovely Sybil seemed to be anywhere near to catching the poor demented beast, Harry obliged with a masterly timed ‘loud noise’ in order to keep the hapless creature moving. It was this public-spirited action, based of course, firmly upon the humble porter’s altruistic desire to serve his passengers’ best interests, that earned for Trumps a not inconsiderable accolade from the spectators, not to mention three shillings and seven-pence dropped by the vicar in his rush to get to the front.

Eventually Sybil became exhausted and lay down. Some of the crowd lost interest and moved away. Sebastian Wigby-Dolt, who had been trying, albeit not very hard, to assist her, lay down next to her supine form. The rest of the crowd lost interest and departed too, evidently realising that if what was obviously about to transpire did not scare the horse then it was probably not worth watching anyway.

Gilbert Shenge turned and walked slowly back to the stationmaster’s office. Wiping a tear of mirth from his eye he paused a while to water the flowers in his smart new greenhouse;

a hastily converted brake van boldly marked *'Experimental - Return At Once to Head Office Siding'* which had arrived attached to a goods train the month before and which because of its large clear-glass windows, had caught his discerning gardener's eye.

"Come on Harry," he said to Trumps.

"Pardon?" said Harry.

They sat down and drinks were poured from a bottle of Piesporter '49, a far better year, which had been chilling unobserved by Sir George, but not unforgotten by Gilbert, in a rusty fire bucket by the door. Shenge began to reminisce.

"You know, Harry, when I joined the Mid-East South-Eastern Light Railway in the year of our Lord 1901, the year it opened, Victoria was still Queen over the mighty British Empire and the railway was already completely bankrupt."

Despite (or more probably in spite of) the railway's consistent performance over the years it had remained bankrupt.

"I've always managed to secure a comfortable living whilst at the same time never been a penny out in the Company books. Now you're going to be the stationmaster here, so I'm going to let you into a few little secrets, wrinkles, to help you like..."

Harry Trumps nodded thoughtfully. He was thinking about the Craxton girl chasing that horse. Outside in the lane, Sybil Craxton's horse neighed in fright but the spectators had gone.

Shenge continued to muse about the running of his railway…

Sir George's Tale

"Turn right here," said Dandridge, now feeling fully recovered, comfortable, and relishing the thought and definite prospect of feeling even more comfortable within a very short space of time; preferably with the aid of some shorts before 'time'.

The soot-black and rust Rover turned into the inn yard, largely by itself. Certainly Sir George had very little to do with the manoeuvre since he had never fully mastered the intricate nature of steering. Braking and clutch control could not be said to be his strongest points either; neither had he ever passed a driving test, nor was he ever likely to do so. Indeed it was doubtful if he even held a driving licence since his hands shook so much that he probably couldn't hold anything at all for very long. He was, in the words of Constable Standfast of the local police, 'Qualified by experience alone.'

Narrowly missing a totally innocent unmarried mother-to-be waiting to cross the road, the car ground to a halt in the cinders-covered car park.

"Are you both all right?" Sir George yelled sarcastically.

"Yes sir, thank you kindly sir," replied the girl, Lucy Upson by name, an undermaid at Sir George's old rambling manor house.

Sir George stared at her in amazement.
"No, not you, you careless cow," he screamed, as much referring to her condition as her presence in the road, "You two, Dandridge and Ashe!"

The three men staggered out of the car and into the lounge bar of the 'Flax Weaver and Pheasant'. The landlord, Quentin Philpots, was enjoying a quiet smoke behind the bar while he leered at the delicious Mandy Havers, the young barmaid who had worked for him - some said under him - for some two years since leaving her previous employment at Craxton Hall. Looking at Mandy always made him smoke!

As the arrival of the three already somewhat inebriate customers disturbed his disgusting but nevertheless highly original thoughts he lifted his bloodshot eyes to heaven and said as pleasantly as he could manage, "Good afternoon, gentlemen, I trust I find you well?"

Quentin Philpots was however not a pleasant man; what he had really meant was that it was hopefully a good afternoon for finding them thirsty and well-lined with money to match that thirst. Philpots knew there was something about Sir George, Dandridge and even Sleet-Ashe that always managed to strike a characteristic note in his heart - money!

"Ha! It might be a good afternoon: we'll let you know later," hissed Sir George. "And while we're at it, we're here at this late hour for the purpose of the market and wish to partake of rest and sustenance under the terms of your market licence, landlord."

This last remark was uttered entirely for the benefit of Police Constable Standfast who was seated by the window in the armchair much coveted by Sir George, and who was enjoying a completely innocent off-duty drink and who had absolutely no idea what a 'market licence' was anyway. Standfast became worried; he wasn't there for the 'purpose of the market' so he very quickly drank up and left, spilling brown and mild down his best white shirt in his haste to comply with a law which Sir George obviously knew and he did not.

Sir George, feeling well pleased with the fluent or rather fluid way in which the remark had rolled off his tongue watched him go. He noticed with pleasure that the poor man did not even stop to put on his cycle-clips in his hurry and could not resist an evil self-satisfied smile when the constable's best light blue trouser, seventeen shilling and eleven pence from the 'Army and Navy Stores' caught conveniently in the oily chain.

"Yes," he thought, "I certainly know how to deal with the law."
Sir George was not the local magistrate for nothing.

"Now enough of that tommy-rot," he continued. "Three gins, no, no, doubles you fool, charge us for singles if you like, and none for yourself."
Sir George evidently knew how to deal with Philpots too.

"You're very generous so soon," mumbled Philpots sarcastically under his breath as he turned to fill the glasses from the optic he specially reserved for young men in sports cars in the company of attractive girls, and any other customers he particularly despised. It was the optic which concealed the absolutely transparent glass marble, bequeathed to him by a friendly uncle who had once worked in the bar of the 'Savoy', and effectively dispensed an undetectable two-thirds measure every time to the unsuspecting client.

“What d’you say?” said Dandridge treating Philpots to the wilting look he usually saved for anyone coming out of the Co-op. “I once knew a cheeky bar steward in Bombay...” The old Colonel never missed a chance of using the rudeness of others as a vehicle for his own wit.

Philpots thought quickly, for though he despised the old Colonel, he could ill afford to be without his custom since the sale of twelve bottles of spirits a week represented a substantial proportion of his income.

“I don’t drink much in the afternoon,” he lied in hasty reply.

Fortunately, the general cadence of the sentence proved enough to satisfy Dandridge who replied, “Oh! Right, good show what?”, being secretly rather glad he did not have to relate the saga of the barman in Bombay since it relied for its point upon a somewhat intricate play upon words and the Colonel’s dentures were loose.

The three men collected their drinks, and at Sleet-Ashe’s suggestion, a dated receipt, the latter to be presented to the accounts department of British Railways, was solicited. They paused to leer at Mandy who was struggling with the handle of a particularly stubborn cellar flap that had taken the ingenious Philpots twenty minutes to nail down, on purpose, that very morning and then they sat down. They chose seats close to the window and in a moment Sir George was comfortable in the chair vacated by the corpulent constable just a few moments before. The window seats overlooked the little market street and from there they could stare at the pretty girls passing by, whilst at the same time remain hidden from the gaze of those in the street. From there they could pass many happy hours in discussion of the more important affairs of life. Above all, because of the great ‘William and Mary’ fire screen behind them, between themselves and the bar, they had every reason to believe that they would not be overheard by Philpots; they would not wish to share their secrets with him. Little did they even suspect that their faith in the sound-deadening qualities of the fire screen, purchased by the inn's previous landlords, William and Mary Jones, pledge-signed Methodists who had installed the article in order to protect their sensibilities from the spectre of seeing strong drink consumed was utterly misguided. Through the cunning use of a Victorian ship's speaking tube, craftily concealed in the brick oven on the window side of the fireplace, Philpots contrived successfully to overhear every word. Philpots did not believe in any secrets, except his own!

"Well, I thought it all went off rather well, didn't you?" said Sir George. It was not a question but a statement of fact. Put another way, if Sir George said it, he believed it, and if he believed it, then it had to be a fact. "Yes, rather well," he reiterated, cunningly turning a belch he could no longer suppress into a fit of coughing which nearly deafened the ever-vigilant Philpots, ear to the speaking tube, behind the bar. Sir George's control was so good during the paroxysm that not a drop of gin was lost!
"Oh! And jolly well done Colonel," he added in a moment of rare generosity. "Couldn't possibly have done it without you, old chap."

"Fancy young Shenge working for us for fifty year..." said Sleet-Ashe.

"Fifty-one," corrected Sir George helpfully.

"…Wonder what the blazes he'll do now. He's got no-one; never married you know," added Sleet-Ashe who had not married either.

"Ginger beer eh?" enquired the bachelor Colonel. "I knew a stationmaster in Jodphur who was a bit like that."

“What? No we don’t want any ginger beer, just three more gins, eh what?” said Sir George rather amused by his success at hiking a pun out of a statement of probable fact, not to mention his delight at having managed to say it before Sleet-Ashe did. In the case of Gilbert Shenge however, such an aspersion could not have been further from the truth, as we shall see.

Dandridge staggered to the bar. He staggered everywhere. ‘Sober’ was a word which did not exist in either his vocabulary or his world, he was very glad to say.

“I hope the old chap will be all right...” went on Sleet-Ashe.

“Of course he will, he’s not going far,” observed Sir George watching Dandridge’s uncertain progress towards the bar.

“Still he can’t have saved much out of what he was paid by the railway and he was very honest; the company books for the line were never so much as a penny piece out, you know.”

“Pounds more likely,” thought Sir George as he remembered the frequent coal deliveries to the manor house in the middle of the night through so many winters in war and peace; best Welsh nuts at two and eight pence a bag. “Now if they’d charged more,” he mused, “the Mid-East South-Eastern might just have made a profit.”

Dandridge, now fully recovered from the shock of having to buy a round of drinks so early in the afternoon, and walking in his usual way, returned with three charged tumblers.

“’bout bloody time,” muttered Sir George absently while looking in the direction of Lucy Upson who was at that moment recrossing the road, this time with rather less personal trauma.

As well as the drinks, Dandridge brought news from Philpots that an ambulance had been seen going up the Windunder Road just before their arrival.

“They stopped here to ask the way to Craxton Hall and to collect a crate of beer,” the Colonel related.

“Why doesn’t her ladyship send her man for her Guinness; having it sent up by ambulance seems a bit much, eh what?” reflected Sir George.

Talking of reflections, he had just caught sight of Mandy in the bar mirror but decided rather selfishly to keep the spectacle a secret. “Must be pulling all those pints that does it,” he thought.

“By the way, did you see young Sybil?” remarked Sleet-Ashe. To Sleet-Ashe everyone was referred to as ‘young’. This unfortunate paternalistic turn of phrase he had invented when he had found himself a very ‘young’ not to mention totally incompetent and inexperienced manager dealing with older, competent, highly experienced and most often resentful, jealous, overlooked underlings. His youth had departed but to the intense annoyance of his subordinates the phrase had not: neither of course had his incompetence.

“Yes, what a stunner, eh! Seems like only yesterday that I bounced her up and down on m’knee at the Wykeham-Sitch’s May Ball,” pondered Sir George.

It was not just on his knee that the wicked old knight had bounced her and it wasn’t ‘yesterday’ either but rather the week before when Sebastian Wigby-Dolt had slipped out to visit the ‘China Palace’ as he had put it. Yes, Sir George took pride in the fact that he never missed the chance of a good grope and Sybil was certainly that. The only trouble was that these days he more often than not groped and missed.

"Course her mother, Lady Fiona was the same, you know. I haven't seen her for years though. Poor old mare must be in her sixties, I shouldn't wonder: late sixties probably..."

"Aren't we all?" commented the Colonel.

"You might be!" exclaimed Sleet-Ashe.

At this point the inebriate knight went to the bar. At one point on that brief journey, it did seem to Sir George that it was the bar that was coming in his direction to meet him. He corrected his pace and walked purposefully, for Sir George had a purpose. It was to make the afternoon as pleasant and comfortable for himself and his two friends as possible by reducing the tedious number of time-consuming trips to the bar. Sir George returned from the bar with three large gins, larger than the ones hitherto supplied. Sir George's keen grey eyes, probably aided by the memory that he had recently fined Philpots twelve shillings for a particularly ingenious 'Weights and Measures' offence, had spotted the marble in the gin optic. Philpots, with a genuine embarrassment and a false promise to "speak to Mandy about it" hung a hastily scribbled 'Do Not Use' notice on the honest but never used vodka bottle next to it, and had poured this round from the silver spirits measure, kept for more discerning customers, on the shelf. Sir George did not spot the two sixpences soldered neatly to the bottom of each glittering cup.

Philpots was however anxious to make amends, particularly when our gallant knight reminded him that his licence was due to be renewed in about a fortnight's time, and that Sir George himself was due to preside at the licensing sessions. Yes Sir George was not a magistrate for nothing.

Three bottles of 'Gilbey's' gin were quickly produced at cost price; three bottles of 'export only' gin, supplied free to

Philpots as an incentive to say nothing about a clandestine weekend, by his brother-in-law in the Royal Navy. Now the canny Sir George had seen the pencilled-out utility marks on some of Philpot's bottles before, but had merely concluded that the labels had probably been printed by the prisoners at Dartmoor. Anyway, after his exertions at the bar Sir George was clearly in need of a rest; or rather **the** rest.

"Yes," said Sir George, sitting down rather heavily and consequently knocking the glass '*Wild Woodbines*' ashtray, recently stolen by Philpots from the 'Rose and Crown' off of the table and onto the floor where it smashed: "I first saw Lady Fiona in 1926..."

"Philpots, just clear up this dreadful mess you've left lying around will you," yelled the Colonel, becoming aware of the broken glass some seconds later and genuinely disgusted that a place in which decent people would eat and drink could be left in such a state.

Gulping his gin and pouring another, Sir George's eyes glazed over as his mind's eye recalled the events which had passed more than a quarter of a century before; yet he was able to see those events far more clearly than he could see the actual events around him in the room.

"...It was very late one night; I'd arrived home from a business trip to London. Took all day to get back I remember. Some kind of piddling strike or other I think it was. That's what comes of emancipating women you know…" he added as an aside. "All the buses were being driven by undergraduates. 'bout the only work some of then had ever done, what? Well, when I eventually got to Potters Junction imagine m' shock at seeing a comely young popsie in charge of the engine. Yes, I remember thinking then that it was a jolly good job we'd given the vote to women don't you know..."

Dandridge was experiencing slight problems following the line of Sir George's reasoning on electoral suffrage, but said nothing as he had just noticed Lottie Self fixing her suspender, safe in the knowledge that she wouldn't be seen, behind the hedge opposite. The Colonel decided to keep this shapely spectacle to himself.

"…You see the fireman, Tommy Ackers, had stoked her up…" at this point Sir George just happened to notice the look on the Colonel's face; he had been expecting it, and said, "Stoked the locomotive, you fool, not the popsie, and then he'd downed tools as the saying goes." Sir George had deliberately added this last expression in order to maintain Dandridge's interest. "Well, you know me..."

Both of his companions had at this point to agree that they did indeed know Sir George. "...Always ready to give a bit of a hand to a young filly, particularly such an obviously generous hearted popsie such as this. I thought to myself I'll fire her up, so onto the engine I got. Well we got to Slowmeadow at about two in the morning and I remember that by the light of the station's oil lamp - the oil lamp which always seemed to be on the point of going out - water in the paraffin I expect - I noticed for the first time who the driver actually was..."

At the mention of the paraffin Dandridge silently remembered the everso many gallons of oil purchased from Gilbert Shenge during the late twenties and early thirties in order to run his Chater-Lea motor-cycle. He remembered too that Shenge had given him detailed advice on how to mix just the right amount of petrol and oil with the paraffin both to start the machine and also ensure that the exhaust had the right colour and smell. Dandridge recalled that he'd smelt the same sort of smell only recently but he couldn't quite remember where. The Colonel continued to wonder about the water in the paraffin but since he'd never had any trouble with any he'd bought from the railway, he concluded that the old fool must be mistaken. Then he thought again about the paraffin sales but quickly dismissed the thought as he remembered that Ashe had said that the company books had never been even one penny out.

Dandridge noticed that Sir George was still talking.

Sir George, aware of Dandridge's sudden inattention said rudely, "Are you listening Dandridge, or am I talking in your sleep?"

"...Well the engine driver turned out to be none other than that lovely lady, Fiona Craxton. Now at about that time I recall there was some talk that she had eyes and a bit more besides for a young captain in the Indian Army. If you remember her poor husband, his Lordship, had been so tragically killed the year before in a terrible shooting accident up on the estate."

"...Lord Danvers Craxton used to like going off shooting in the dark, you see. He always said it reminded him of his days in the service of the Raj; tiger shoots and all the rest of it. You'd know all about that sort of thing, eh Colonel?" added Sir George quickly continuing before any reply could be forthcoming.

"...Well, it was about six in the morning that they found him. It seems that he had tripped and fallen sometime earlier that night and that some soil had lodged unnoticed in the barrel of his twelve bore. Now it seems that he hadn't noticed this - too pissed probably 'cos they found an empty bottle next to the body - and when he later came to give the cook's cat both tubes, just before dawn, the gun burst and killed him outright. He used to have his cartridges made specially for him locally, you know, with special high percussion powder, so he really didn't stand a chance..."

It was at this point that Philpots, who had been hovering nearby for some minutes muttering plaintively something about one pound thirteen and seven pence, made the startling revelation that Gilbert Shenge used to make special high-velocity shotgun cartridges in his spare time at the station.

Sleet-Ashe, recalling the line's extraordinary propensity for fog decided that henceforth all the fog warning detonators used on the Mid-East South-Eastern Railway would have to be counted far more regularly.

Sir George paid up and the landlord of the 'Flax Weaver and Pheasant' shambled off.

"...Well, her Indian Army chappie didn't come home so very often and of course I sympathised and took the opportunity to tell her that I came home quite often. She suggested that I came home with her, there and then, and quite often afterwards. So I did and…well we're all men of the world aren't we? Need I say more, what?"

From his position behind the bar Philpots wished Sir George would say more; Philpots was smoking again.

"...Still it's just as well the General Strike didn't go on a bit longer or I might have had to marry her, eh! Had a nasty moment at the end of it though."

"At the end of what?" asked Dandridge looking at Sir George's still open flies.

"Shut up!" hissed Sleet-Ashe.

"...Saturday night it was. I'd just finished firing her up from Potters Junction and to tell you the truth I was looking to a pleasant evening firing her up at Craxton Hall so to speak, when, don't you know, I turned round to find her smack in the arms of her young soldier: I'd just carried that Indian Army blighter home. 'Thank you Ackers, that will be all', she says to me, and he gives me a five rupee coin for my trouble and thanks me for the smooth ride: my smooth ride I remember thinking. Here, look, I've still got the damn thing. I've still got it after all these years." And with that he displayed the coin, green with verdigris, bearing the head of Queen Victoria on one side and on the other the entrails of a dead, probably drowned fly, which had clearly had the misfortune to depart this life in an alcoholic haze after having entered Sir George's pocket with his wet change some time earlier, in search only of some tasty morsel.

"...Never really saw her again. Twenty-five years ago it was. She nodded at me from time to time in passing, but that was all. Heh, are you alright Dandridge? You look a bit pale; Philips, Philpots or whatever you call yourself, bring us some brandy; not a glass you fool, a bottle, a bottle. Say, did you ever meet her? No, not Mandy, everybody's met her..."

Sir George had noticed that Sleet-Ashe's attention was wandering and had followed his gaze to where the nubile Miss Havers was bending down and Philpots was warming his hands.

"Not Mandy," he said more loudly, "Lady Fiona…"

Sir George was aware of a previously unseen nostalgic gleam which had appeared in the eyes of the General Manager of the East South-Eastern Region of British Railways and for a moment began to wonder whether beneath that urbane exterior there lay hidden the lusts and perhaps even secrets of a 'real man' as the Colonel would have put it.

There did!

Sleet-Ashe's Tale

From behind the bar something snapped. It was not as Sleet-Ashe had hoped the sound of Mandy Havers' suspender elastic, neither was it the sound of Philpots gently chastising his erring barmaid for her transgression with the gin optic. It was merely Mandy making quite sure, at least temporarily, that the landlord of the 'Flax Weaver and Pheasant' should, as she so succinctly put it, "Keep his filthy wandering hands off of her!" by means of the simple but nevertheless highly effective expedient of shutting his fingers painfully in the bar flap.

"Bravo! That caught the bounder!" muttered Sir George who just happened to be looking that way at that moment whilst wondering why his brandy had taken more than the three seconds he had allowed for it to reach him. He was rather glad too that they were not his fingers that had suffered though.

"And you can behave too," added Mandy as she brought him the bottle, "I'll not have the likes of you laughing at old wandering mitts when he's only doing what you'd like to, given half a chance!"

Mandy had gifts too. Two gifts actually; well five if you counted her other more obvious attributes: one was a well-developed knowledge of how to deal with Sir George and practically anyone like him, and the second was a profound self-awareness and confidence concerning her three other attributes and how they might be used to her best advantage. It was, after all, this that had resulted in her early expulsion from the Nightwell Academy for Girls, not to mention the untimely resignation of that nice Mr. Touchman, her teacher.

"Sorry I'm sure," said Sir George, suddenly sitting up having bent down to retrieve an accidentally-dropped pipe which he had let fall at the precise moment the short-skirted Mandy and the brandy arrived.

"That's all right, sonny boy, I'll forgive you," said the delicious Mandy, stroking Sir George's bald head: she always liked to give her customers hope after she'd admonished them. After all it was always good for tips.

Mandy swayed provocatively back to the bar, watched droolingly by Dandridge, Sleet-Ashe and Sir George. Each hoped that she would perhaps trip and fall over that ruck in the carpet and settle once and for all the rumours that were rife about her sartorial secrets.

"Well, I did meet her several times during the year 1926..." said Sleet-Ashe.

"Who, Mandy? I shouldn't have thought she was even born then," commented Dandridge, his mind very much on other things. Mandy's three things to be precise.

"...No, Lady Fiona Craxton I mean. It was in the course of Railway business, just after the General Strike I remember it was. We were having a bit of trouble with the 'push-pull' on this line…"

"Too much of it going on in the carriages on the dark winter nights was there? Caused by eating too much cheese you know," Sir George added helpfully with an odd look on his face. He was still perspiring joyfully from his encounter with the barmaid.

Ashe ignored this deliberately obtuse comment coming as it did from the past chairman of the Railway who should have known better; even if, as Sleet-Ashe frequently suspected as he looked through the minutes of past board meetings, he didn't. He allowed himself a few moments of glorious revelry before continuing.

"...I was working in the District Superintendent's Office at that time. Well, one morning the bell rang and I knocked at the great man's door with trepidation. I wondered what I'd done or not done. I was greeted with a smile however. He asked me to get down to Windunder double quick and sort the whole thing out. You see it was like this…"

"Yes, come on, get to the point," said Dandridge thus effectively delaying the start of Sleet-Ashe's story by a further few seconds.

"…When the line was originally built we ran into rather a lot of trouble in the form of the third Lord Craxton. The third lord, Viscount Zenith Craxton I believe his name was, refused both the building of the railway and the running of trains unless he could exercise some considerable degree of personal control over them. It happened in lots of places up and down the land, particularly in Scotland. Now you're probably wondering why a railway which was already so terribly short of money bothered even to build a station at Windunder at all: after all it is six miles from anywhere and the only building that's there apart from the station that is, is Craxton Hall. Come to think of it," mused the General Manager, "I wonder why it's called Windunder at all."

At this point the Colonel farted loudly in order, he thought, to give Sleet-Ashe the clue by which the little mystery might be solved. Ashe ignored it for a few seconds but then was forced by circumstances to open the window.

"...Well, it turned out that he'd only let the line go ahead if the Company agreed to build him his own personal station, with its own personal signal box, controlling his own personal signal. You see you have to have a signal box to control the signal," he added by way of a totally unnecessary explanation. "As it turned out we needn't have even bothered for the silly old duffer died during the opening ceremony of the line though it was agreed by all that it was rather a pity that he didn't pop off before..."

Sleet-Ashe paused, quietly thinking, but not saying, that he was secretly rather glad that Zenith Craxton had not died before the completion of the line since had that been the case then he would never have met the lovely Lady Fiona at all. All this he thought with a leer so intense that it would have instantly transmogrified Max Miller into the Archbishop of Canterbury!

"At the inquest into his lordship's death it was noted that the water which he had drunk with his Scotch in the refreshment room of the station had been tainted with some 'Brasso' from the signal box. The coroner had said that 'the Brasso must have accidentally got tipped into Craxton's glass from there, the main water tank being just behind, and that it was extremely fortunate that no-one else seemed to have been affected. We never did find out just who had had the accident with the metal polish but it is interesting to note from the Company records kept during those early days that Shenge was frequently complimented for the spotless way in which he kept his lamps and signal levers shining. I still have my doubts about that 'Brasso'," he added tellingly.

“What in the name of the Railway has all this utter nonsense got to do with you meeting Lady Fiona?” asked Sir George, as much to show the other two that he had been listening to every word as for any other reason.

“...Well years and years passed by and everyone on the Railway forgot all about the line’s grace and favour stopping rule. The rule of course was still retained in the rule book and all new employees of the Company were tested on it. Then some months after the death of her poor husband, and most likely inspired by Lady Fiona’s new-found love affair with all matters concerning the permanent way fostered by her sterling work during the General Strike, for some inexplicable reason she began to stop every single train. Every single train, day and night for a whole week, was held up at her signal, by her ladyship herself, for up to an hour or until she said it could go. For every complaint or word or even look of abuse she received from any of the delayed passengers or worse still one of the Company’s loyal servants she would keep the train standing there for another five minutes. It is still very well documented on the line and of course recorded carefully in the signalman’s log book that the quality of language of the present Bishop of Bognor Regis, who was at the time speeding back to his wife from a pastoral visit to an afternoon tea-dance held in the home of a young widow, resulted in a delay of some four hours! You see the engine could not pass the signal with it set at danger or the driver would be in error of the rules and would face losing his job...”

At this point the General Manager reflected that a more likely explanation for the driver not wishing to pass the signal at danger was the prospect of plenty of overtime spent waiting.

“…You see, only she possessed the clearance for the passage of the train once she’d set that signal. Because of the dear Lady Craxton…” and as he uttered the word ‘dear’ his eyes glazed over and tears began to form in their corners, or it may have been a splash of gin from the Colonel's glass as he slipped from his chair in a convulsion of laughter brought on by the vision he'd allowed himself to have of the Bishop, "…and because of that dear lady trains were held up from Land's End to John O' Groats."

"There are no trains at Land's End, never have been. You could wait all day and all night for a train there and never catch one," spluttered the Colonel who had always maintained a strict regard for the truth and no regard whatsoever for geography after having discovered that warring tribesmen had once drawn maps with south at the top in order to confuse the British and therefore had tended to hold battles where his troops were not!

The Railway General Manager did not even hear this aside as he was at this time fully occupied in self-congratulation. He had managed to introduce, quite successfully he thought, the notion of the importance rather than impotence of this piddling little branch-line to nowhere within the affairs of the national transport system of Great Britain.

"...It was only after the local Whig M.P. the Honourable Randolph Shifte, particularly late home after a particularly stringent French lesson with his French mistress, blamed his delay, by way of explanation to his recently emancipated wife, upon the short-comings of the railway, and questions posed largely to add verisimilitude to that excuse, were asked in the House, that I was sent up Craxton Hall to straighten things out."

"What did you want to do that for?" asked Sir George who rather liked the idea of a Whig having to explain such things to his wife, not to mention the idea of several dozen passengers, delayed on the workmen's special, having to explain their lateness to their disbelieving employers and probably having their wages stopped into the bargain.

"...You see, in order to change any of the conditions for the working of the line it would be necessary first to obtain an Act of Parliament. Such 'Railway Orders' are obtainable only at great expense - the Company's expense - and since the line was already bankrupt we simply could not afford it. This I carefully explained to her ladyship one afternoon in 1926. She quickly understood but suggested that in return for her promise to cause no further delay to trains on the line she should be pressed to some small token in return..."

"I bet you wouldn't have minded pressing her to a few tokens eh?" mused Sir George with a grin.

"...So from my trouser pocket I took one of these…"

"Put it away Ashe, now there's a good fellow; There's no need for that sort of thing; now I know you've had a few but not in public, eh?" yelled the Colonel in alarm.

From behind the bar Mandy stood on tip-toe to see if the rumours spoken about the General Manager were true.

"...No, not that you fool, this!" And with that Ashe produced from his pocket what looked like a gold coin secured to his watch button by a very substantial chain. "This is a gold pass and it is usually given only to retired railway general managers and the like. It enables the holder to go anywhere on British Railways and pay nothing whatsoever for journey or service."

"Well, I must go on a journey now, and I won't be paying. Get some drinks Ashe, there's a good chap. Scotch this time if you don't mind, Ballantine's mind you, if that cretin's got any; what's good enough for Queen Victoria is good enough for us, eh what?"

When Sir George returned, his drink was waiting for him and his flies were still undone.

Sleet-Ashe continued... “So I suggested to Lady Fiona that such a gold token should be accepted as showing the Company’s humble gratitude for her kindness in not necessitating the complete revision of the 1926 ‘Bradshaw Railway Timetable!...”

“Time, time; who’s calling time: what nonsense, besides it doesn’t apply to residents, and we’re residents. Philpots, Philpots, damn it all where is that confounded man? Ah! Here you are at last. Philpots, fill up some beds, I mean put the barmaid to bed, I mean put Mandy to work making some beds; after all,” he added as an aside, “We’ll soon be too pissed to move with any luck.”

“All right, Colonel, sir,” said Philpots, remembering the time he had spent as an officer’s batman until he was caught stealing whisky: he’d missed the marks on the bottle that canny young first lieutenant had made after turning the thing upside down first. He mused that he’d never been caught for watering it down though. Philpots stopped thinking about his army service and immediately began thinking of two other things: of the pound notes he’d be able to charge for rooms that would never be used - he knew full well that the three sots in the bar would never be able to get up the stairs; and he thought of Mandy, bending over making the beds. “Yes sir, right away,” he said as he went off to supervise matters personally. Shortly afterwards, outside a horse neighed loudly in alarm.

“...Well, that seemed to solve the problem…”

“Not really, the fool will be back in a moment,” interrupted the Colonel who thought that this remark had something to do with the landlord of the inn.

“Oh! I don’t think Philpots is as quick as all that, still he is a bit younger than we are,” rejoined Sir George.

"...At least it solved the problem for the time being," continued Sleet-Ashe. "And for the rest of that glorious afternoon at Craxton Hall I enjoyed tea, a pleasant view and idle conversation..."

"Bloody hell is that all?" cried Dandridge and Sir George in unison.

"...I considered that I had acquitted myself, on the Company's behalf, rather well. All went well until the annual company dinner later in the year. The port had been passed, the ladies had retired to do whatever ladies do after they've retired, and the glorious smell of mild-cured Havana filled the air…" Ashe thought to himself how lyrical he could be in the haze of nostalgia. He thought too how strange it was that the light fitting above his head seemed to be swaying rhythmically. "Must be the Scotch," he thought.

"...As I was saying gentlemen, the guests were smoking so I excused myself and went to visit the Royal Doulton suite if you know what I mean. Well, who should I meet there but Lady Fiona Craxton. I was very shocked and I told her so; I told her very quietly actually for I did not wish to wake old Admiral Saltlean whom I suspected was fast asleep in one of the cubicles judging by the snoring noises, not to mention the empty rum bottles which had rolled under the door. 'Well,' said Lady Fiona, "You said that the token you gave me meant I was allowed absolutely anywhere on the railways', and with that she pushed me into one of the cubicles, locked the door behind her and….well we're all men of the world aren't we! Put it this way, she showed me many tokens of her affection during the rest of 1926. I haven't seen very much of her since then, though, except sometimes during routine visits of inspection to Gilbert Shenge's five stations. She was often there. She used to buy her vegetables and eggs from Shenge personally. Always picked them up herself. He must have had a very large and well-kept railway allotment in order to be able to grow all the stuff she bought for the hall, that's all I can say. The goods trains he made up were never an item short you know."

Suddenly there was a loud scream from the room above, followed almost immediately by a large bang as if something or somebody had either fallen or been pushed to the floor.

The horse outside neighed in alarm once more and a few seconds later Philpots lumbered into the bar red-faced and sweating profusely.

Dandridge considered that Philpots had been remarkably quick while Sir George considered him not to have been up to par for the course.

Philpots was obviously embarrassed and the Colonel feeling a moment's pity together with the realisation that the afternoon was fast moving towards that unpleasant interregnum between the closure of the inn's market licence and the opening of evening hours said, "Drink up chaps, it's my round, three more Scotch's for us, and have one yourself Philpots. Join us for it if you like. Just the one mind you, just for the one..." The old colonel had remembered only just in time the rule about not ever drinking with the other ranks.

Philpots' Tale

Philpots brought over his glass. The Colonel and Sir George noticed with some considerable delight and not a little longing that the landlord had also brought a bottle of Ballantine's twelve-year-old malt, that it was as yet unopened and that it bore the customs seal of the old king. This was a joy to behold and no mistake. Now if Philpots managed to leave that bottle behind after he'd finished his one drink then all would be well. Very well. Philpots sat down and very soon four glasses of that pale gold water of life were shining in all their goodness and glory upon the table.

All of a sudden, to the shock and consternation of those present. who were fully expecting, if not by their very demeanour, demanding that Philpots should drink up and shut up, the landlord of the 'Flax Weaver and Pheasant' broke the silence. Even Philpots himself knew that he was treading a very dangerous path indeed and in such company he did not usually speak until or unless he was spoken to. He knew his place; it was either counting pound notes, putting glass marbles in optics, experimenting with his soldering iron, or experimenting, in his mind at least, with Mandy…

“...Course you know I knew her ladyship too…” He looked about him but his eyes met only a stunned silence. The stunned silence however shouted ‘continue’ at the top of its voice.

“...I was post-boy at the village sub-post-office and I could be called upon at any time of the day or night to deliver parcels, letters and telegrams…” Philpots was always at pains to stress his indispensability, even at an early age. “The post-mistress Miss Haste sent for me one November afternoon. It was getting late I remember. I was to go quickly up to the Hall with an important letter. I had to walk because I had lent my G.P.O. bike to Mandy’s father, a clergyman I fancy he was, who needed it to get to Potters Junction and for some reason did not want to go on the train...”

At this point Philpots became aware of a sneaking suspicion that he should not perhaps have revealed what he knew about the parentage of the comely Miss Havers. His audience were finding it almost impossible to contain themselves. All three were bright red in the face and seemed not to be breathing at all. It was only their reverence for the cloth and the fact that they did not want the likes of Philpots to see the likes of then finding such things of amusement that prevented an outburst of laughter seldom if ever heard within the hallowed walls of the ‘Flax Weaver and Pheasant.’

“...It was getting very dark and a thick swirling green fog made it most difficult for me to see the road or to find the way up the lane to the Hall…”

Sir George was only to ready to agree that the Windunder road was a very easy place to be lost on. After all he’d been lost there on a number of occasions though usually in the company of his retriever, leather game bag and twelve bore. Usually out of season too.

“…I began to feel rather frightened...”

“What, frightened of the dark, wretched man, frightened of the dark were you, eh,” rambled the Colonel who had only just cured himself of that lifetime diurnal fear by means of the simple expedient of sleeping with a ‘*Price’s Palantine Nightlight*’ in a saucer beside the bed.

“...It was not just the dark and the fog that frightened me, gentlemen. You see was very frightened by the letter I was carrying. You see, I’d never seen anything quite like it before. For one thing it did not bear a postage stamp…” Sleet-Ashe considered there was little unusual in that since he frequently posted letters without them. Usually for the same reason he forgot to sign or date cheques. He always put a little gum on the stamp-corner of the envelope though to make it look as if a stamp had been there. Sleet-Ashe became aware that Philpots was continuing. “...and for another it had the Royal Warrant impressed upon the back…”

It was here that the Colonel became genuinely impressed by the fact that Philpots should even know what a Royal Warrant was. The Colonel only knew because he’d seen one on his Indian Army commission and also on the label of the Ballantine’s bottle in front of him.

“The letter also bore the words, ‘From the Office of the Lord Chancellor of England and Wales’. I thought it must be something important.”

Here, with a profound sense of relief, the old Colonel knew he’d been wrong about Philpots; the man was an idiot after all. Dandridge felt better almost at once.

"...When I got there the footman showed me right in to where her ladyship was resting. She was very, very beautiful I remember thinking. Well, Lady Fiona could see that I was very frightened, I was shaking you see; then she came over and put her arm around me to calm me down a bit like. As I rather liked having her arm round me I decided to shake all the more..."

"Disgusting!" shouted Dandridge, "We used to stop that sort of thing in India with plenty of exercise, Bromide in the tea, and cold showers at dawn; that was when we could get any bloody water anyway."

"...Then Lady Fiona opened the letter. I remember waiting for a reaction of anger or shock but all she did was roar with laughter until the tears were quite literally running down her cheeks. You see the letter turned out to be an instrument of annulment of her marriage to Lord Danvers and he'd died more than a year before. After a while, the Lady Fiona stopped laughing and dried her eyes with a silk handkerchief that seemed to fill the whole room with its lovely scent. She looked across to me and smiled. She said 'The fog is getting very thick. I think you'd better stay the night here. I'll have a bed made up for you in the servant's quarters.' She said I was to go back in the morning if the fog had cleared by then. Now in those days, before the war, one had to obey one's betters and respect both their ideas and their wishes..."

"Quite right too," exclaimed Sir George who had long considered that since he had no betters he didn't have to respect anybody, their ideas or their wishes. He also considered that that made him better than anyone and therefore everyone had both to respect and obey him; well at a pinch just obey him: he'd settle for that. Yes, he'd settle for that, he mused as he looked at Lucy Upson who had just sat down rather carelessly on the bench opposite.

"...We were also taught that any idea a lady or gentleman had was bound to be a good one. Anyway, I thought that spending the night at Craxton Hall was a very good idea indeed and when Lady Craxton told me she would send word of my safety by way of the train, I said I would be most happy to stay. Of course it did not occur to me that I could have gone back home on the train just as easily..."

"...Her ladyship was kindness itself and I was treated to probably the best meal I had ever had, oysters I think they were, and way past my normal bedtime I was taken to the servants' quarters and made comfortable. Later that night, just before midnight, when the whole house was sleeping and in darkness, Lady Fiona came into my bedroom, just to see if I should need anything and to set my mind at rest over one or two matters. 'I think I'd better explain to you just what an instrument of annulment is,' she said. I'm afraid I pretended to be not very bright and during the course of that night the lovely Lady Fiona had to explain it to me several times... Still we're all men of the world, aren't we?" concluded Philpots.

"You bounder!" cried Sleet-Ashe.

"Bravo!" shouted Sir George, though even he would have found it difficult to know just why he had shouted it.

"Let's have another drink," said Dandridge, who had been the first to bring his sense of outrage under control and to realise that in spite of it all life would have to go on. He was also eyeing the bottle of Ballantine's which looked to be in danger of departing behind the bar with the landlord.

"I'm very sorry sir," said Philpots with a pained expression on his face. He looked at his watch and shook his head. He'd also thought he'd heard a groan from Mandy in the bedroom above and had decided that it was probably time for tea; or to be more exact

- forty; position forty! "I'm very sorry, gentlemen, but it's after hours."

"Rubbish, utter rubbish!" roared the Colonel with feeling, hastily looking at his own watch which fortunately for all concerned at the battle had stopped prior to the Battle of Kurristan some thirty years before, earning him the nickname of 'Bridgelately', not to mention saving all their lives into the bargain. "Rubbish!" he roared again with a voice so loud this time that it almost caused Lucy Upson to miscarry. "We're residents, and anyway it's before hours!"

And the sheer incontrovertible logic of the old soldier's argument settled the matter once and for all. Philpots brought the drinks, and then with a realisation that, tale told, he'd been dismissed, went upstairs to see how Mandy was getting on with the beds. To the chagrin of the three remaining in the dusky bar he remembered to take the twelve-year old Balantine's with him.

The Colonel mused once more that Philpots was probably not such a fool after all.

After the landlord had gone, Sir George in a rare moment of caring thought he could see in the old soldier's eyes a deep look of wistful sadness.

"Did you know her ladyship, Dandridge?" he asked gently of his old friend.

For a few moments, not in time but spanning the years and experiences of a lifetime, there was silence, and then in a quiet voice Dandridge replied.

"Yes, as a matter of fact I did; rather well actually."

There was silence once again as he reflected privately upon those moments in his younger days which may best be described as pure, impassioned, unbridled lust!

The Colonel's Tale

"Yes, I did know her," he said again, "In fact for a time she was the very apple of my eye. She was the reason I never married, you know; I mean what woman could follow her…"
"My God, what a lovely reason," thought Sleet-Ashe.

"...It was like this. You see, as a young man I was commissioned into the Indian Army. I just had to be, you see, I mean I had all of the necessary qualifications for it…"

"Yes, and none for anything else," thought Philpots from behind the bar, his right ear adopting almost prehensile characteristics in its desire to consume the speaking tube on his behalf.

"...Yes, all the qualifications: a father in the church or practically anywhere else there were choir boys, a pass degree from a non-conformist university and a simple but consuming love for three things in life: beating servants, polo and fencing."

Sir George began to wonder why it was he never joined the Indian Army for he quite liked beating servants too.

"...Well, very soon I became fed up with the first two, there was so much of it around so to speak, so I turned all my attention to the latter, fencing." Ashe looked up but the wily old Colonel was expecting it. "Not that sort of fencing, not the stuff that goes round your rotten little stations, I mean the stuff you do with sabres and foils and cutlasses; the stuff I had all the qualifications for. One of m' loves…"

"What qualifications?" thought Sleet-Ashe who wisely then decided to remain silent since it had suddenly occurred to him that he had absolutely no qualifications for anything and that Sir George probably knew it."

"...Mind you," continued the Colonel who was just beginning to get into his stride, or in his case, shuffle. "The railway does have considerable significance to my story, yes a definite connection as we shall see." Dandridge smiled at this point and wondered whether he ought to explain his pun. "No," he thought, "My tales are so good that the pun will become self-explanatory..."

At this point he was interrupted by the laughter of Philpots who had just spotted the pun.

"...Well apart from routine patrols and the odd servant-beating there really wasn't a lot to do…" At this point Sir George, who had seldom, if ever, done a day's work in his life, and fully believed it to be something other people did, expressed his heartfelt sympathy and understanding. "Anyway, myself and a brother officer by the name of Danvers Craxton - see the connection - decided to form a fencing club. You know, to give the officers some other pastime when they were bored stiff with beatings and such like. That was in about the year 1919 or so. We were both young subalterns then and never been kissed by either the girls or each other, eh what?"

Sleet-Ashe, who had once had the profound misfortune to be kissed by a bearded uncle not to mention his equally bearded aunt immediately wondered what it would be like to be kissed by a subaltern, but his thoughts which had already thoroughly disgusted him were further disturbed by a comment by Sir George. "...Talking of kissing subalterns reminds me that I once kissed a pilot officer during the war." This he announced with a contrived look of shame upon his face. The statement was followed not unexpectedly by a shocked silence from his friends. This was what he had hoped for. "Yes, it was rather pleasant actually." More shocked silence and Sleet-Ashe eased himself imperceptibly away from Sir George's side. "Yes, it was in the blackout during the war. I was fire watching and when the incendiaries started to fall I went down to the shelters to hide, I mean shelter; well you couldn't be too careful could you, and as a fire-watcher I was indispensable don't you know? Well when I kissed this Air Force type it was a mistake, you see; as I turned to kiss my sister goodbye at the end of the raid I caught this pretty young WAAF a real smacker instead. It was much better than kissing that bag of a sister of mine, I can tell you..."

Sir George didn't have to tell them that. At various times both Dandridge and Sleet-Ashe had been treated to a view of that dreadful spectacle, the Honourable Gertrude Slagge. As Ashe put it whimsically "She was of the stuff of which nightmares were made."

Sir George's silent friends breathed again. They felt they could continue to remain in Sir George's company without any danger of being subjected to any 'gross indecency of an unnatural kind' as the Colonel would have put it.

From behind the bar came a snigger from Philpots. He had heard the story of the kiss before; from his sister, the pilot officer.

Sir George suddenly realised that he had so rudely interrupted the worthy old man of action and said, "Come on Dandridge, get on with it."

"...Well things at the fencing club went along pretty well for a time but after a while it all became a bit boring. You see the sport became too safe. After all, you couldn't really chop a man's head off and then expect him to sit down in the same mess with you for tiffins afterwards, now could you?"

Sleet-Ashe considered the possibility and agreed that indeed it would be very difficult.

"...I mean you got dressed up in all your clobber and thrashed at each other with a blunt sabre or whatnot. If you were lucky enough to hit a chap it didn't matter 'cos you couldn't really hurt him. No, not even if you thrashed him hard..."

Not for the first time that day Sir George thought of thrashing and then of matron. He pondered upon the image for several seconds, reflecting that though he'd often been thrashed he had rarely if ever been foiled. He was about to express his thoughts which he happened to think rather witty when Dandridge continued.

"...I suppose you could have given a beggar blood-poisoning but that was all you could do..."

Sleet-Ashe was lost. He simply could not understand why anyone should want to give a beggar blood-poisoning since he had always considered that beggars probably had enough to put up with already. Feeling that he might have missed a vital part of the story, he kept his thoughts to himself since he did not wish to appear foolish.

“..They were a bit rusty you see; not the beggars, the sabres. Anyway the safety lark became rather boring. Interest declined and the fencing club became less and less used. I decided to liven things up a bit…”

“I wish you’d start with my glass. Now that could do with a bloody liven up and no mistake,” suggested Sir George and as if by magic Philpots arrived with a bottle. “He must have read my mind,” said Sir George, though he did not mean it since he believed that Philpots probably couldn’t read anything, let alone minds.

“...I knew a chap near Calcutta who could read minds,” said Dandridge and did mean it. Sleet-Ashe was by now completely lost and made a positive decision to listen more carefully in future. “...In the summer of 1920 or was it 1921 I got a nasty touch of Punjabi Elbow Wart: chaps all over India were dropping like a whore’s drawers with it they were. Anyway I decided to take some sick leave back home. Well as luck would have it I got on the wrong train at Potters Junction: pissed I expect I was, and ended up at Slowmeadow in the middle of the sodding night. Pouring with rain you see, sodden! Worse than the ‘black hole’ it was; no lights, no buses, no buggers to carry cases, no beggars to kick, or was it the other way round, and no pub open. Well I was standing there just wondering what the hell I was going to do when I heard this noise behind me. I turned round and wished to God I’d got my white-man’s frightening stick with me. ‘Good evening sir,’ says an obviously well-meaning voice, ‘Can I be of any possible assistance to you?’ It was head porter Gilbert Shenge. Well I did not like to ask him to find me a beggar to kick so I told him I’d settle for a cup of tea. So in the middle of the night I find myself drinking m’ Mazawatee in cosy conversation in the station-master’s office. We passed the night in interesting conversation about the British Empire; Shenge must have been abroad at some time I remember thinking, very knowledgeable…”

“Isle of Wight probably,” muttered Sir George wrongly. Still Sir George probably believed that the ‘Isle of Wight’ was abroad since he had never visited another country in his life and even believed that the ‘Isle of Grain’ was in Scotland.

“…Having told me I should have to wait for the first train in the morning, at five I think it was, we talked of other pursuits. Well it seemed that young Shenge was very skilled with his hands and could make almost anything from metal. By the end of my sojourn with him he had agreed to make and then hone a sabre so sharp and fine that it would take the balls off a bat in full flight…”

Ashe wished he could think of expressions as explicit and succinct as those of the Colonel, but then as he was acutely aware, he had not had a University education.

“…It would be ready by the time I was to return to India. At the end of the month my elbow was nicely healed and I could once more hold a bar-side gin without too much discomfort - something which really mattered - and return to India, which didn’t. Yes I could hold my gin once more…”

“Except when the glass is empty,” commented Sleet-Ashe as usual mistiming his observation to his own disadvantage.

“Ah! You’ve noticed, fill them up then, there’s a good chap,” said Sir George who was always rather more careful about the timing of his comments.

“...When the time came I revisited Slowmeadow to collect my sabre: the craftsmanship you would have had to have seen to believe and I marvel even now after all these years how such a thing could have been fashioned, without even the minimum of equipment, from an old length of rusty, disused rail...”

At this point Sleet-Ashe decided to make a check of the amount of disused rail available within the region and to estimate the number of sabres it would be possible to make. After a second or two his keen brain spotted a problem; he would have to find a railwaymen who was also a swordsmith and as far as he knew there was only one with the necessary expertise and he had retired that day. He gave up the idea.

"...Throughout the long sea journey back to that jewel of the British Empire I tried to conceive of a way in which such a devilish awesome weapon could be put to the purpose for which it had been designed. How could it be introduced into the routine of the fencing club? The more I considered the problem the more I came to the conclusion that all my plans to return a little excitement to the mundane affairs of the club would be frustrated by conscience. You see, there was nobody in the whole of the regiment whom I disliked sufficiently to want to wound in a slashing manner: beat yes, wound no. Well the razor-sharp sabre upon which I had pinned so many of my hopes I'm afraid served little purpose. It was hung up in the mess where it was of no use at all except as an innocent talking point. It was set alongside the regiment's other trophies like the drum we used to scare the snake-charmer's cobras. Yes there it stayed gathering dust, though not fortunately or unfortunately gathering, as we shall see, gathering any rust. Now remember that this razor-sharp weapon had lost none of its fine sharp edge. So there it was hung in the mess for all to see and there it stayed for years; almost forgotten it was. Forgotten until one sad day when something most unusual happened. Something both tragic and so long it doesn't happen to you, totally hilarious. It was in April 1922. The regiment had found itself engaged in a minor war somewhere or other. I can't really remember now where it was and I doubt if I knew then. Our losses were very great indeed, so much so that it became necessary to commission men from the ranks. Terrible thing that, changes the whole tone of the mess, lowers it for one thing if you know what I mean. Still on reflection most of the acting-subalterns thus commissioned got killed in the fighting and so were no further trouble to us after that, if you get my point. Well my talents for leadership had around that time been fully recognised and I was made a captain which gave me the opportunity of leading the fighting from a desk in H.Q. At about the same time Private John Smith, not even spelt with a 'y' or an 'e' applied for and was granted, though by God knows who, a king's commission in the Indian Army. He was made up to an acting subaltern too and by God he started acting up almost at…"

There was a brief silence as each of the three friends took a drink; the prospect of thinking about Smith did not bear thinking about.

"...Now you remember Danvers Croxton, well he came into the mess one evening and spotted Smith, whom he'd made a habit years earlier of kicking at every opportunity, sitting in the corner. Now Danvers was very proud of the regiment and all its standards and traditions. After all you couldn't have someone who was used to being kicked doing the kicking could you? Danvers greeted Smith in the manner he used for all subalterns commissioned from the ranks. 'I see we have our privates on show in the mess' I think it was. Or some other friendly time-honoured cry. Poor Danvers, he was not in the best of moods, since earlier in the month he had been involved in a particularly bloody skirmish lasting about twenty seconds or so during which he had attempted to rescue a young Indian girl from a fate worse than death at the hands of an Afghan from over the border. Ran him through he did. Unfortunately at the inquest it turned out that the man was the woman's husband but that Danvers could not possibly have known this. In the fight poor old Danvers had received a black eye from the bounder and suitably qualified by that experience decided quite rightly to take it out on Smith. Smith of course, due entirely to his lack of breeding, took exception and suggested immediately that they should go to the fencing club and settle matters between them once and for all, to sort the whole thing out. 'You can't do that, you're not a member,' I remember the adjutant saying, but on that point the adjutant was wrong. Earlier that very day, Smith, anxious to become more fully involved in the life of the mess, called at my office to enquire of the possibility of becoming a member of the fencing club. I remember thinking at that moment of the sabre behind the bar. Here was an opportunity not to miss. I had already tried unsuccessfully for several days to get the young bounder killed by sending him out on only the most dangerous patrols, in order to give him good fighting experience, but the young stench kept coming back. Yes, the fencing club provided just the opportunity I was seeking. After letting him plead with me for several minutes I finally gave in and let him join. It was to be a painful decision in more ways than one, I can tell you. I thought of Shenge's sword and all it could do as I gave the blighter his membership card. Well Smith was anxious to fight and so was Danvers. There was really no stopping either of them. 'Let's go now, I really can't wait,' said Danvers as he grabbed Smith warmly by the throat and dragged him, feet off ground, out of the crowded mess, by his ear. 'You'll need a sword, here take this one, it's been here for years and has never been used,' said Danvers. I tried my best to warn Craxton of the danger several times during the walk to the club but his blood was up and he would have none of it. I remember his saying that by giving Smith the old weapon it would give him the edge. It certainly did! Off to the club went all ranks; commissioned ranks that is. Couldn't let the others see us fighting, could we? With the first thrust the inevitable happened and poor old Danvers was cut off in his prime; or rather his prime was cut off! At the court of enquiry it was all put down to the most terrible accident and no blame was attached; but we court-martialled Smith anyway for having a dirty uniform button during a battle the day before, reduced him to the ranks and booted him out. He changed his name I did hear and had a son who I believe keeps a pub around here some place..."

It was at that moment that Philpots fully appreciated for the first time the difference between his father's surname and his own and the value of a shortened birth certificate. He didn't know whether to laugh or cry, so did neither. He had hated his father too much to care at all.

"But you still haven't told us how you came to know Lady Fiona," said Sir George.

"Shut up and I will," Dandridge testily replied.

"...In 1923 Fiona and Lord Danvers Craxton were married. No-one thought to tell the poor soul about his lack. Honour and trust of the regiment, and all that, what? In 1924 I was invited by his lordship to spend a summer leave with them up at Craxton Hall. I'd been promoted major with a small command of my own, up by the Afghan border, I think it was…"

"That explains why there was an increase in trouble in that area at that time," thought Sleet-Ashe who had had a brother who had served as a fitter in the Royal Air Force and who had married a recently-widowed Indian girl whose husband had been killed on their wedding night by a demented Indian Army Officer.

"...It was the first time I set eyes on that fair flower of youth and I was fortunate to become a regular though sometimes secret visitor to Craxton Hall after that. Later, after I was promoted to half-Colonel which at that time meant a home posting to the War House, after that poor blighter Danvers had got himself killed, I was able to offer the odd touch of comfort to the dear creature so to speak…"

"...Mind you, that girl had spirit, real spirit; did you know that during the General Strike she was an engine driver… I wonder what she's doing now?"

Dandridge looked up. He had expected some reaction to his last comments, but now he saw the reason for their lack of interest. Sir George, Sleet-Ashe and Philpots had each fallen into a drunken stupor.

"Oh well!" said the old soldier, "Time for a piss."

A few minutes later having suitably refreshed himself with a glass of Ballantine's twelve-year-old filched from the landlord's own bottle; taken from his own hands. Dandridge thought for a few seconds about what Lady Fiona might be doing at that moment and promptly fell asleep too.

Lady Fiona's Tale

And what indeed or rather what 'in' deed was Lady Fiona Craxton doing up in Windunder at the ancient seat of the Craxtons, Craxton Hall. Well it may be said that up at the hall, the party was in full swing. Lady Fiona and her companion for the day, an imported young French chef from Brixton by the name of Pierre Sang-Froid were really enjoying themselves. Actually this was not strictly true. To put it more exactly, it was the Lady Fiona who was enjoying it, while Pierre Sang-Froid, to the intense satisfaction of his wallet rather than anything else, was supplying it.

In recent years, more especially since her constant companion Mandy, now barmaid at the 'Flax Weaver and Pheasant' had left, Lady Fiona had been forced more and more to accept the paid favours, rather than the more genuine attentions, of companions such as Pierre. To put it even more plainly, since the delicious Mandy had left, Lady Fiona, whose own not inconsiderable former beauty was beginning to fade, was finding it increasingly difficult to seduce young men. It often seemed to her that such standards in society were falling; in her youth, she remembered, simply being in close proximity with a titled lady would have been enough, or even for a young colt just to be near such wealth. Even the latter she was enough of a realist to accept. But now it was increasingly evident these things were simply not enough. It was disgusting, but she had to admit that nowadays young men wanted to be in possession of some of that wealth if they were to impart any favours at all. Being a woman of the world, and anxious no doubt to do her bit to aid the period of post-war expansion which the British public so obviously awaited and deserved, not to mention help the re-establishment of the entente-cordiale, which she had been informed at finishing school was by no means a drink consumed with iced water or lemonade by wayward Frenchmen playing petanque at a Boy Scouts camp, but rather an international feeling, she did the only thing that a woman of her position could do. She was forced by her reduced circumstances to negotiate simple transactions involving money. After all, she had always believed that it was sometimes necessary to pay for good service and had long since made up her mind that having paid, she would make quite sure it was well served.

The morning had broken fine and clear. Outside, above the dewy glade, the first blackbird greeted the golden morning. Lady Fiona had been awakened from her slumbers at the sound of the first birds. This immediately frayed her temper, since in her dreams she had been about to seduce for the third time that handsome pretender to a now defunct European monarchy to whom she had been presented at Buck House just the month before.

“Sod the birds!” thought Lady Fiona.

Beside her bedside rested a small silver bell. It looked remarkably similar to those bells used by the farmers on the Isle of Skye to identify sheep on the hillsides. It was. You see, during her frequent but secret visits to Skye, it had often seemed to Lady Fiona that the use of such bells would have been rendered unnecessary if the consumption of ‘MacLeod’s’ eight year old Scotch whisky by the islanders could have been reduced in some way. This would have allowed her to obtain more of the stuff and to enable the sheep to be more easily spotted by less inebriate shepherds. Anyway she’d stolen the bell during a wartime holiday on Skye some years before. But before her crime is considered too heinous to contemplate, it must in all fairness be stated that after she’d removed the bell she’d helped the farmer by locking the hapless ruminant that had carried it in the crofter’s own privy.

Lady Fiona rang the bell. She was looking forward to her breakfast which with any luck would be a demi of ‘Moet 36’. After slightly under two seconds she rang the bell again; breakfast was taking a devil of a long time to arrive. Where the blazes was her faithful old retainer?

Lady Fiona was having to wait. And as she waited she remembered with a smile that this was a very special day. Gilbert Shenge was retiring. She rang the bell again.

“Shit, where is that man?” she cried.

This time, in only seconds, the door opened and Sybil Craxton, her daughter, entered the sunlit room. Thoughtfully and wisely Sybil carried the champagne. Lady Fiona smiled first at the bottle, noticing that just the right amount of condensation was forming on the outside of it, and then at Sybil.

Sybil informed her mother that for some reason she had been unable to rouse Lionel since he had locked himself in the servant’s loo on account of the day. With instant recall Lady Fiona realised the significance of Sybil’s last remark. It was indeed an important day in the calendar of Lionel. The first Tuesday of the month; the day the old fool’s continental magazines arrived by post, having been carried into England in the diplomatic bag of Caruthers Barrington of the Foreign Office.

Lady Fiona, having generously offered to show her daughter how naughty French women drink champagne in bed said, "I'll fix the queer old josser. I'll teach him to do his reading before breakfast - my breakfast that is. Sybil, go and make the front door ring and then tell him it's the police come to see him about complaints by the other users of the public conveniences in town. Go on, off you go, dear," said Lady Fiona with a winning smile.

For good measure, she gave the little silver bell another hearty ring. She was feeling better already. Sybil returned, her lovely face bearing a similar smile of amusement to that of her mother.

"Now Sybil, I should like you to do one or two little things for me today. I have a feeling that I may have to lie down for a bit this afternoon," she added. She always laid down for a bit; Lady Fiona was after all somewhat of a conservative with regard to positions whilst nevertheless remaining liberal at the same time! "Now, I'd like you to attend the presentation at the station on my behalf. Shenge is retiring this afternoon: it's at Slowmeadow station."

Lady Fiona had already planned her day and in no way did it include listening to boring speeches made by bored and boring people. She would not be attending the presentation to the venerable stationmaster as she had other fish to fry. Well, strictly speaking they were not fish, but oysters and they certainly would not be fried.

Sybil departed more or less at the same time as Lady Fiona's old retainer Lionel entered the room. Despite his age he had been agile enough, he thought, to give the local police the slip. Escaping through the loo window he had entered his lady's bedroom by way of the French doors. Unfortunately in his haste to vacate his reading room - an inaccurate description, since he only ever looked at the pictures - he had not been too careful about where he put his feet and consequently stank strongly of 'Brobat'.

"You rang, my lady?" he enquired.

"Not within living memory," replied Lady Fiona with a smile that could only be described as pure sunlight.

"How droll, my Lady," whispered Lionel.

"Now Lionel, I'm finding it increasingly difficult to get a man…"

"I know the feeling, madam," replied Lionel Gaye sympathetically, his own luck in that direction being similarly on the wane.

"I want you to go into town and telephone 'Fortnum and Mason' and order five dozen oysters and have them sent up here today. Quickly mind. And then I want you to get in touch with the 'Adonis Agency', no not the 'A.A.' you old coot." She had noticed that Lionel was taking notes, "…and tell them to send along their most experienced young French chef to serve them to me."

"Yes, my lady; will that be all, my lady?" Gaye knew perfectly well that the serving of the oysters would definitely not be 'all', but he said it anyway.

"You know damn well that it won't be, now clear off," said Lady Fiona with that look of love and affection she usually saved for the little man from the Inland Revenue, who, having found himself on one occasion face to face with the smile of a loaded elephant gun, tended to keep his social calls to a minimum.

Lionel Gaye minced off. He took with him the copper-solder copy of the gold railway pass that he'd skilfully forged in an idle moment. It was surprising how useful it had become and how much better he was treated by those nice young porters when he showed it to them; the pass that was.

Lionel stumbled down the deeply rutted lane to await the arrival of the morning train in Windunder station. The birds in the trees were still singing loudly.
"Sod the birds!" thought Lionel, "If they'd not woken Lady Fiona I could have finished my first magazine." Gaye did not care for birds of either kind.

The little steam train came into the station, almost over-running the uneven platform even though it had been built to accommodate twelve carriages. This was strange since the longest train ever to run on the branch was just two coaches in length. In truth the footplatemen were so shocked at seeing a passenger at Windunder that they almost forgot to stop. No-one got off and Lionel got on, seating himself in the corner of the 'ladies only' compartment.

Gaye mused upon the glorious fact that as soon as his task was completed he would most certainly not be needed for the day and could therefore enjoy himself to the full; it was a pity he'd had to leave his fine examples of French literature behind though, but he knew that to carry them about in public was a risk he could not take. Still he knew that nobody could possibly find them at the Hall, concealed as they were in the false lid of the 'Thomas Crapper Original Pattern Patent Water Closet". Little did he even suspect that at that very moment, back at Craxton Hall, Sybil was busy with the poster paints she saved for making church notices, adding intricate and highly original designs to the illustrations in Gaye's latest delivery.

The train lurched into Muttering Market and Gaye, remembering the breakfast-time visit from the police and consequently feeling somewhat uncertain about the presence of a stranger in a military-style raincoat on the platform, got out on the line-side and made his egress by means of a hole in the wire fence: the same hole by means of which the man in the raincoat had gained access to the station, in order to avoid paying his fare, some moments before. Gaye then was not followed and just a few minutes after his arrival, his tasks completed, was to be found imbibing happily in his favourite seat in the ladies' bar of the 'Witt's End' public house.

His seating position in this noble establishment had been chosen with that special kind of care that comes from long experience, since from his seat Lionel had an almost uninterrupted view of the three things in which he was most interested. His window seat overlooked what may best be described the 'Clochemerle' of the East; he could see the entrance to St. Boniface's Elementary Boys School; and he could see the young potman behind the bar who always assured him of his best attentions. Yes he felt safe in the knowledge that even his humble talents would not be needed at Craxton's that day. He drank the second of the 'Watney's Stingos' he had lined up waiting on the table in front of him.

Lionel watched the mid-day train arrive and his trained eye saw the porter turn a passenger round and direct him back onto the train. "That'll be the French chef," mused Gaye. "Now I wonder if I could turn him round…"

Meanwhile back at the Hall, after a journey lasting two and a half hours, one hour from London to Muttering Market followed by ninety minutes and three punctures for the three miles up the private lane to Craxton Hall, the van from 'Fortnum and Mason's' was arriving with Lady Fiona's oysters.

Lady Fiona then, as usual, refused to pay for them, citing the delivery van's lateness and mentioning the name of a very important person indeed if you happened to be employed by 'Fortnum's' and wished to remain so. The drivers were not tipped and the van departed. Shortly afterwards the doorbell rang again.

With that feeling of exhilarated expectation Lady Fiona rushed to throw open the door. She needn't have bothered for her jubilant feelings turned quickly to abject nausea as she saw that the door framed that congenital idiot Sebastian Wigby-Dolt, her daughter's mindless suitor. Though he was young, and she thought probably male, there was no way she would even have contemplated him: she didn't want him anywhere near her, and as a woman of the world, 'near' was a word she would use to describe any distance less than three hundred miles. Sebastian, for his part however, always displayed the characteristics of a grovelling faithful dog towards her and her lovely daughter Sybil.

Fiona gave him her sweetest smile and swallowing hard said in a joyous tone of welcome, "Hello Barstie!"

Fiona really did not know what it was her daughter saw in him; except that he was probably worth at least twelve million pounds. During two world wars his father, the late Cobley Wigby-Dolt, C.B.E., had been responsible for the sole manufacture of an item of equipment vital to the allied war effort. It was that single flat brass button worn under the belt of an officer's tunic in order to keep the belt flat. Made for threepence, and sold to the War House for one pound and ninepence, protected worldwide by letters patent, a fortune or even a fivetune had been made. A fortune that had been rather well invested.

Sebastian's father had met his demise on the last day of the war while conducting personally the field trials of a new flat brass button designed for the officers of the A.T.S. It seems that due to faulty stitching at the tailors, the brass flat fell off the A.T.S. girl's tunic and into the old fool's gin and tonic and in seconds he'd choked. Died on active service, Sebastian always said.

"Now Barstie, you're just the man I want," she lied.

"Rather!" uttered Dolt in an accent so far back that it couldn't help but meet itself coming forward on the way out and was thus rendered entirely incomprehensible.
"Rather!" said Dolt again, thinking for a brief moment that his luck in the direction of Lady Fiona might at last have changed.

"Now, Barstie," said Lady Fiona, desperately trying to get his full attention for the third time in as many seconds and musing about the appropriateness of her pet name for him, "I want you to take the Rolls, meet the mid-day train, collect my French chef, bring him back here, and then go to Slowmeadow and look after Sybil."

"Rather, rather, rather, rather, rather!" uttered Wigby-Dolt who had cunningly noticed that in Lady Fiona's request there were in fact five separate commands and had decided that it would be both polite and original to acknowledge each one in this. His reply also served to cover up his fundamental lack of vocabulary, but did little to conceal his lack of mathematical ability since there were in fact six instructions in Fiona's request.

Wigby-Dolt stood for a few seconds smiling; in fact he was smiling while he was thinking and he was thinking desperately to remember what it was that Lady Fiona had asked him to do. Dolt was not very good at thinking and generally smiled to cover his ineptitude in that direction. Lady Fiona could wait for his thought processes no longer since she found that Sebastian's smile only added to the general nausea she felt for him, so with a cheery wave of her first two fingers she said, "Good, then bugger off," and slammed the oak door firmly in his face.

With a crunching of gears that the yeoman craftsmen of Derby would never have thought likely or even possible, Sebastian Wigby-Dolt managed to draw the 1932 Mulliner out of the barn. Unfortunately the rear bumper had chanced to catch upon a straw bale. The straw bale in which Lionel Gaye had made his second hiding place, and the morning's breeze served to carry to innocent and unsuspecting readers throughout the county, literature the like of which was never to be found in the 'Boots Penny Library'. Indeed Lionel Gaye was particularly pleased with the photograph which happened to float down the chimney of the 'Witts End' but wondered whether he'd seen it somewhere before.

Within a few minutes the Rolls returned more or less intact; remarkable since Dolt, who had been educated in France, if you could call it an education (or Dolt even educable), had never driven before, either in Britain or anywhere else for that matter.

A white-faced Pierre Sang-Froid stepped shakily from the car which Dolt then proceeded to reverse into him, depositing the young chef squarely in the deepest part of a duck-dunged puddle in a way hardly likely to fit his attire for the purpose of being presented to a titled English lady. Pierre grovelled to his feet and then fell politely to his knees.

"That's not the last time you'll be on your knees today, sonny," said Lady Fiona, treating Pierre to her most rampant sexual leer and helping, or rather dragging him into the kitchen. "Today is a special day for me," she imparted as she carefully sponged the trousers she had already removed from Sang-Froid; "It is the twenty-fifth anniversary of a day twenty-five years ago. A day in 1926," she added.

The logic of this was entirely incontrovertible but was nevertheless lost on the poor Frenchman from Brixton who had at that moment spotted both the oysters and the bed. He wondered why he had ever left the fish and chip restaurant owned by his mother at Southend-on-Sea.

His worst fears were soon to be proved all too true, as, with a movement so sleek, graceful and polished that it would have favoured either Pavlova or a Windmill Girl with an itch, Fiona bolted the door, hid the key and presented the bewildered chef with a book entitled 'The Aphrodisiac Nature of the Mollusc' and a recipe from a banned continental guide suggesting '60 Interesting Things to do with Oysters' which had been secretly imported in Caruthers Barrington's diplomatic bag the week before. How Fiona had managed to wait for a whole week she would never know.

During the course of the afternoon she was to experience 59 oysters which 'worked' so to speak, together with one that was to poison her in a manner so acute that it was ultimately to take her ladyship's life.

Thus it was that groaning in pain, yet tinged with a feeling of rare delight, Lady Fiona whispered in the ear of the distressed chef. Pierre Sang-Froid was at that moment experiencing pangs of self-recrimination, not to mention an uncertain feeling that he might not have washed his hands properly before the preparation of the seafood.

"You must get a message to my solicitor, it's very, very important indeed," she groaned. This she said with a smile on her face that even in this most extreme of moments she just could not seem to get to go away.

And so it was that Clarkson Brookley, L.I.B., University of Port Said, arrived at the Hall to supervise the addition of a codicil to the will of Lady Fiona; a codicil which prior to that had left her will unfinished.

This was the moment that Clarkson Brookley, born Terry Brown of Balham, had longed for, as it would give him a little time in which to supervise some further additions on his own behalf. Seven and one half per cent of several millions would do him very nicely. He would be able to buy himself a new law degree which would be just as well since the Law Society was currently investigating his present one. “Mind you!” he said to himself, “Seventeen and a half per cent would be better and odd marks have been known to appear on wills before now…”

While Pierre Sang-Froid was out summoning the lawyer, Lady Fiona had bravely and not without some considerable struggle, managed to rise from her death bed. She managed too to open and consume three bottles of Moet ’38 which she always kept slightly chilled for emergencies such as this. “The last vintage before the war; pity to waste it. I might not be able to persuade ‘Fortnum and Mason’s’ to deliver where I’m going and you can’t trust the post,” she said to herself.

And in the haze she joyfully relived the serving of each of the fifty-nine oysters and remembered with stoic affection the sixtieth too. “Yes, that one had definitely been the best for all that,” she mused. Lady Fiona remembered too the other nights of long ago when the man she loved most of all in the world had impassioned her days and brightened her nights. Fiona was for a moment sorry that their plans would not now come to fruition.

The doctor, whom the young chef had thoughtfully summoned at the same time as the lawyer, confirmed the worst. The end was certainly very near. A kind of peaceful expectant silence filled the darkened room, until with a cry of “Let’s have a bar-b-cue!” Sebastian Wigby-Dolt and Sybil burst into the kitchen.

Lady Fiona signed the codicil of the will, grimaced at Wigby-Dolt and faded from this life; still with a wicked sexual leer on her face and a simple counting lesson for Sebastian on her fingers.

"I'm rather sorry," uttered Dolt as the ambulance made its noisy arrival in the yard outside. It had just collided with the Rolls which had run away down the hill owing to an unset handbrake. Dolt had been keen to display his new-found prowess at the wheel of a motor car to Sybil, but had so far been unable to find the rein with which to fasten the thing to the fence.

Quickly recovering his composure he added, "I'll ride with her to hospital in the ambulance; it'll pass the pub and the butchers so I can buy the booze and the sausages for the bar-b-cue on the way."

Clarkson Brookley quietly left the room. He was carrying the codicil of the will away to be copied prior to its formal reading in the great library that night. He was wondering about the other amendment he was going to make; seven to seventeen: shouldn't present any problems, third time this week!"

Brookley used the top of his silver-quilled pen with considerable dexterity to force the lock of the drinks cupboard and with a largesse never before witnessed, treated all the servants and the drunk-returning Gaye to all they could consume during a 'happy hour' that was to last well into the middle of the next morning.

"With all the Hall inebriated, no-one will see me at work," said he.

Mandy's Tale

Back in the quiet bar of the 'Flax Weaver and Pheasant' at about this time, the nubile Mandy was preparing to make her move. It would be an event for which she had long been preparing, and the stories which she had overheard in the bar of that public house during that sunny market afternoon of reminiscences had served to convince her that the time was absolutely ripe.

Mandy had been born in the area, on the wrong side of the sheets as the old saying goes. Her mother had kept an afternoon tea-room complete with afternoon tea-dances. Her father was unknown to all but a very few people, though there were however some still living nearby who said they could remember a man all dressed in black who used to pay the tea-rooms more frequent visits than most other patrons and whose face bore an almost uncanny resemblance to that of a certain well-known Bishop.

Mandy's mother had, notwithstanding, had a profound influence upon the developing character of her little girl, and by the time Mandy had left school at the age of fourteen she had already acquired a fine reputation. More accurately a 'fined' reputation since it was widely rumoured that she had already been fined by the local magistrates on a number of occasions. In fact it was because of her reputation that she had to leave school in the same way as she would probably have to get married one day - some locals said in the pretty near future if Philpots had anything to do with it - others said she probably would have to even if he didn't.

Once she had left school she had found it very difficult getting a job; she never found it particularly hard to find employment though. The trouble was nobody wanted to employ her for more than a few minutes, which, after all, was as long as she ever wanted them to employ her! There were some employers of a respectable nature who would have given her work, but most of them had watchful, canny wives who were unwilling to have anyone with the obvious charms of Miss Havers around. Thus it was out of pity for this poor innocent girl that Lady Craxton, at that time in her fifties, offered Mandy employment as a lady's companion at the Hall up at Windunder.

Lady Fiona was glad to have such a pretty thing around her. After all, pretty things often attracted other pretty things and sure enough Mandy was frequently visited by swarms of pretty young men. "Pretty young men with their pretty young things," as Lady Fiona had once remarked. You see there was something about young men that Fiona liked and it certainly wasn't Brylcreem.

For seven years the relationship had worked remarkably well. They had been true companions, sharing meals, secrets and sometimes… well we're all men of the world aren't we?

Two years before the day in question, she had left her employment at Craxton Hall following an unsuccessful attempt at extorting money from a well-thought of old retainer whom, she discovered, had some thoroughly disgusting habits. Mandy had been most surprised by Lady Fiona's attitude in taking her servant's side but would not have been had she known that her ladyship had used the threat of exposure to avoid paying Gaye any salary for more than twenty years. Still, when Mandy left the hall she had taken with her some small items which she had every reason to believe would prove cast-iron investments.

She had quite genuinely found by accident, but quite deliberately kept, Lady Craxton's personal diary for the year 1926.

After making quite sure that the men in the bar were sleeping soundly still, Mandy went quietly up to her room. Standing on a stool in a way which just a very few minutes before would have had Philpots either smoking or even totally in flames, she took down a dusty case. This she place carefully on the bed before unlocking the same with the small silver key she kept on a fine chain round her neck. Carefully she opened the case and removed the white tissue paper which covered its contents. Having folded the paper she took out a dress and paused to smooth it carefully with her beautifully-manicured hands.

The dress, or more correctly gown, was of a fine, pure white, almost diaphanous silk. It was a gown that she had borrowed, with her usual over-developed sense of community property, from her ex-employer and companion Lady Fiona.
"The ugly old cow won't miss it," Mandy had thought, but had Fiona lived for just one more day then this would not have been the case; Fiona still had plans for that dress.

Mandy put the gown on; just the gown, nothing else. She had, she knew, to create just the right effect. That gown, she knew, would be very well-known indeed to the four men sleeping soundly with their dreams and memories in the bar below. It was the gown in which they were each, so to speak, entertained.

Slowly she closed the case but did not replace it on the top of the cupboard, as she had spotted the window cleaner leering at her. She wagged her finger at him three times, turning the third wag into a slightly incorrect version of the well known Churchillian gesture. The window cleaner turned hurriedly away, soaking Lucy Upson as he slopped filthy water from his bucket.

Mandy looked at herself in the mirror marked 'Property of the North British Hotel' which was screwed to the door. She was pleased with the result; pleased to note too that she bore an uncanny resemblance to a youthful Lady Fiona. This she knew would heighten the effect she wished to create.

Mandy went to her dressing table and carefully removed the bottom drawer - the one which always has a recess underneath where women often hide those treasures which they wish to keep, yet keep secret from their husbands and where of course husbands, upon their honour, would never think of looking.

Philpots never looked there but then he'd only ever been married for one night after which his new bride, disliking his penchant for nocturnal acrobatics, had left him to enter a convent. Poor Philpots had been forced to enjoy his honeymoon in other ways above a chip shop in Southend. The thought of that honeymoon, Mandy remembered, had often made Philpots' blood run cold.

From that space under the drawer she took three other very valuable items which she had also purloined. The diary, a copy of Lady Fiona's last will and testament, completed up until about that time, but with one small part that she had been unable to find, missing, and Sybil Craxton's birth certificate.

Mandy Havers crept down to the bar, neatly avoiding the stair which creaked and the one which Philpots had loosened on purpose, in the hope that it would cause a trip which he could turn to his advantage, since Philpots always conspired to be at the bottom of the stairs whenever Mandy went up or down. She moved stealthily behind the bar so as to be precisely on hand at that most precise of moments. She watched and waited till the sleepers stirred.

And in the haze of their half-sleeping, half-waking, each of the men became aware of a white clad figure moving serenely in their midst. The shock was immediately too much for Sir George, who, relying on an instinctive neuron response rather than clear vision and manual dexterity which he never possessed anyway, managed to pour himself another drink, drink it and pour another.

"Now boys," said Mandy, "It's time for my story, so shut up and listen. As you all know Lady Fiona is very rich and very kind, and, as you all know too, she and I were companions. Well during those years of companionship we got to know each other well, very well. Some things we discussed, some things I found out, and some things, gents, I will not hesitate to make up..."

"I hope you're not saying I wear make-up young lady," said the Colonel who was now fully awake.

"...Quiet, or it'll cost you even more," cursed the lovely Mandy ominously. "Well, while I was sorting through her ladyship's things while she was on holiday on some Scottish island during the latter part of the war I think it was, I came across three things which I thought might come in very useful one of these days. This was some time before I left her service to make my own sweet way in the world…"

As she uttered these words she toyed idly with the hairy mole under Sleet-Ashe's chin.

"...Well here they are, dearies, or rather copies of the three things that mean so much to all of us." Mandy had spotted Philpots eyeing the fire and she knew from experience just how quickly those hands could move. "The three things are a diary for the year 1926, copied from the one in Lady Fiona's fair hand. A diary from just twenty-five years ago, General, a birth certificate pertaining to a bouncing baby girl, Stoker George and a will with some interesting names in, Mr Cinders.

All three had heard their respective nicknames before and each disliked his intensely. Each had the feeling that he would find even more to dislike before the afternoon was over.

Mandy felt rather proud of the way in which she had put the first stage of her statement over. She had only to add her not unreasonable demands, the demands which each of the three men knew inevitably would come, and her foolproof plan would be complete.

Mandy continued. "...Yes, I thought these might come in useful. Now let's take the diary. Well, I'm pleased to say that though you're four drunken old sots, you are truthful at least, and the diary confirms all that you've said this afternoon..."

"And a good bit more besides," thought Sleet-Ashe.
"...And a good bit more besides," added Mandy as she read correctly the mind which was causing the reddest face she'd seen since Philpots' early that afternoon.

"...Now, this is interesting too," continued the erstwhile barmaid. "It's young Sybil's birth certificate..."

"Well, there's nothing compromising in a birth certificate," said Ashe, who knew all about birth certificates. He'd got one; the only certificate he had got in fact."

"...Hold your noise, Clinker," said Mandy politely. "This certificate is interesting in that it shows Lord Danvers Craxton as Sybil's father despite the fact she was born in 1927: now that's two years after the old bugger died and a year after the instrument of annulment which showed he couldn't possibly have been even if he was." Mandy had added her last convoluted exactitude simply because it amused her. She continued: "Now that must have been the longest pregnancy in the history of the world, particularly since the old eunuch died a year before the instrument of annulment was drawn up anyway..."

Sir George mused at the mastery of the mathematical art displayed in one so young. It rivalled even his own, but he had a sneaking suspicion that this was going to be the least of his problems. Sir George did not of this occasion think of matron. He had a shrewd idea as to what was coming later.

"...The third useful thing I managed to get hold of is a copy of the will. You will see that half of the Craxton family fortune goes to Sybil in trust from her father, whoever he might be, when old Lady Leatherface herself snuffs it. Yes Sybil gets half from her dear old dad..." repeated Mandy who chose this particular moment to stare at each of the four men in turn. Each man remained silent and each turned bright scarlet. "...Now you will see from the copy of old wart-cheeks' will that the rest of the estate is subject to a rather curious division; each one of you fine upstanding gentlemen shares just one fifth of the remainder. That's about a cool quarter of a million each. 'Course that leaves two fifths of the entire estate unaccounted for. It seems that this amount goes to a beneficiary named in a codicil which I couldn't find..."

"Pity," mouthed Sir George, Sleet-Ash, Dandridge and Philpots in unison. Probably the very first and very last time they would do anything in unison in their lives. Each of the men was by this time in no doubt as to what in a very short time would be happening to them and each thought that it was indeed a great pity that Mandy had not been able to find out the name of the fifth man, since then she would probably have picked on him and left them alone.

“Shut up!” mouthed Mandy and immediately the four took a sensible salvation in silence.

“...Now then, each of you gentleman is a man of some considerable standing; though I wouldn’t mind betting that you’d have some difficulty standing now, and not because of the booze, though God knows that ought to be enough. Each of you holds a respectable position in this community of ours...” Sir George went pale, his worst fears were realised, he had heard this preamble before, as evidence in a blackmail case he’d once heard on the bench. “…Each of you took amorous advantage of a recently-widowed and vulnerable woman, the impressionable Fiona, though I’ll grant you that with a woman of her appetites you really didn’t have much choice, and consequently each of you might be the father of that dear sweet Sybil. And now gentlemen, each of you will make me out a cheque to the value of a quarter of your legacy. I have the precise Stock Exchange valuations should you need them. Cheques payable to me in cash if you don’t mind, the four of you…”

Surprisingly the four men acted in unison again, three times more in fact. There were four sudden intakes of breath, four glasses were clutched followed almost immediately by the simultaneous clutching of four wallets.

Sir George thought of his eight boardroom sinecures in the city, five of them in religious publishing; Sleet-Ash thought of his doting maiden aunt whose firm oddly enough supplied all the coal for the East South Eastern Region and who read each Sunday with shocked delight the most salacious cases reported in the ‘Empire News’ and the ‘News of the World’, and who had already cut half the family out of her multi-million pound will for comparatively minor transgressions such as showing a white light in a blackout and having an inefficient silencer after it had been deliberately sabotaged by a drunken reveller on V.E. Day. Dandridge thought he needed another piss; and Philpots wished he'd not watered the Scotch.

It was Sleet-Ashe who broke the silence. "You've certainly got it all worked out, haven't you?" Mandy smiled and began to nod towards the open cheque books. The smile did not last long and the cheque books were very quickly closed and replaced in pockets.

The silence and gloom which had fallen on the room so jolly in reminiscence just a few minutes, before was shattered by the bell of the cream-painted Daimler ambulance. There was a squeal of brakes, the opening and slamming of a door and in rushed a breathless Sebastian Wigby-Dolt.

Philpots did not even have time to lift his eyes to heaven, nor mutter his customary platitudes before the young man blurted out, "The Lady Fiona has died and three bottles of 'Johnny Walker' to take away please. Dolt paid and rushed out, and for a brief second, during which time Philpots locked the till, there was silence.

"...Right, you can put those cheque books away, boys, the will'll be read tonight and I'm going to find out who copped the forty percent and get to him before anybody else does..." It was the dulcet tones of sweet Mandy.

The Colonel marvelled at her way with words; the very precision of her language impressed him greatly, not to mention that his bank account was now more or less reprieved.

With that she ran from the room at a speed she never used for waiting customers but often employed when the landlord was chasing her. Followed closely by Sleet-Ashe, Sir George, Dandridge and Philpots, Mandy pitched through the inn door and up the market hill to Muttering Market station, rushing in order to catch the evening train to Windunder.

Several people struggling home with newly-acquired possessions turned to see if Mandy's white silk gown would be blown up by the breeze, or better still be caught by a briar, but sadly all were disappointed. Only the booking clerk at the station was pleasantly surprised. He sold five tickets to Windunder, and since he knew that Mr. Sleet-Ashe, would never believe such an entry in the returns of ticket sales, and since he knew too that his worthy manager believed him never a penny out in the Company books, he decided to save trouble for all concerned and simply pocket the fares.

After what seemed like an age and almost certainly was, the 'Up Market Day Mixed Goods with Passenger Brake', as it was shown in what passed for a timetable for the line, arrived at Windunder and five passengers, the only five occupants of the passenger section of the train, scrambled out. At first they all ran and then they trudged up the pot-holed lane towards the Hall. The Colonel wisely remarked, remembering the small fortune he would soon inherit, that it was probably not worth busting a fetlock, since their loot was once more intact. Obviously only Mandy hurried, for her, speed in money matters was of the very essence: always had been!

When they got to Craxton Hall they found the fine oak doors wide open and the party in full swing. They were treated to a barrage of drunken cries from the servants who clearly knew how to treat the passing of their mistress with the due deference it deserved. Lionel Gaye, remembering his purpose in life, beckoned them in and then went back to doing, rather unsuccessfully due to the amount of alcohol in his system, something quite obscene to the footman. Leastwise he thought it was the footman; in fact it was the undermaid but after realising his mistake Gaye came to the shocking conclusion that he had quite enjoyed the experience and had obviously been missing something all these years.

"Now, there's a turn round for the book," he said to himself.

The family solicitor, who by this time had finally decided to settle for a mere eleven and one half percent of the estate led them into the great library and carelessly shut the door. The oak door slammed equally carelessly on his forging finger bringing tears to his eyes and pain to his bank balance.

"Good," thought Dandridge, particularly pleased at seeing Brookley in pain. "That'll teach you!"
Dandridge had recently had recently had a relative's very valuable will proved by Brookley and had ended up owing money on the deal. Strange that.

Lady Fiona's will was read. There was nothing new there. The four men looked at each other with considerable relief and not a little puzzlement. Then with all the solemnity the occasion deserved the codicil was opened. 'Two fifths of the five million pound estate was to go to Gilbert Shenge, the stationmaster, her most generous of friends, deepest of lovers, most tender of confidants…'

Several people present at that moment would have liked to have shown Gilbert Shenge exactly what to do with his tender... Mandy, silent and unobserved, left the room. She had work to do! Work at which some had said she was very good. Work she had from time to time in the past even quite enjoyed. Work at which she was quite simply a past master, or more accurately mistress. Work which simply had to be done before the postman arrived with Shenge's copy of the will.

Mandy knew that, despite her many talents she could not delay the Royal Mail, though she had once managed to delay a well-known European Prince for several pleasurable hours during one of his visits to Craxton Hall.

Mandy made her way back to the little station and re-boarded the little train. The same train, since it had been held against the signal that Lady Fiona's ambulance had triggered as it lurched, driven by a Guinness-besotten driver, over the Windunder level crossing some time before.

After an hour's deliberation, a delay which was to have far-reaching consequences to the British Railways working timetable for 1951, the train was flagged across the completely empty level crossing to make its seemingly endless journey to Slowmeadow station. Except for Mandy the train was completely empty as was usual. But then it always had been!

Gilbert's Tale

By the time that Mandy had arrived at Slowmeadow station, Gilbert Shenge had finished his musings upon the most profitable, for him, means of running the affairs of the railway, not to mention the effective organisation of Slowmeadow station. He had explained most carefully and painstakingly to Harry Trump's unhearing ears the intricacies of paraffin sales, the fabrication of motor spirit, the watering and weighing of best Welsh nuts, the machining of rails, the medicinal uses of metal polish, the safe and effective dismantling of railway fog detonators, double-entry book keeping in two sets of books, multiple animal husbandry and the gestation period of livestock, the shipment of vegetables and perishable produce and generally the thousand and one things that every good railwayman worth his salt should know if he is to run the railway to the mutual satisfaction of both servant and served, probably in that order, without ever being so much as one penny out in the Company books.

His third bottle of Piesporter was empty. Lady Fiona always drank that year he recalled. Shenge was aware too that Harry had gone; well, he thought he had gone anyway.

"The young just never listen to good advice," he said to himself.

Shenge did not even notice the arrival and departure again of the market train, he just didn't care. He had finished with the railway.

Then, on this his retirement day, through the haze of late evening and the haze of the wine as well, to the tuneful accompaniment of the ticking of his retirement presentation watch, (already three-quarters of an hour slow), and the clicking of the death-watch beetle, (getting quicker by the minute), his lovely lady, as he had been expecting, came to him, and he was treated to a night of passion seldom if ever recorded in the annals of the 'Railway Gazette'.

For out of the gloom, highlighted by the guttering flame of the platform hurricane lamp as it burnt uncertainly on a mixture of three parts paraffin and one part water, there came to him, he thought, his lovely Lady Fiona. All his joy, all his very life personified; the very soul of his being, not to mention object of his all-consuming carnal lust.

And there in and on that very evening, they would begin to recapture and share that part of their lives that would last for ever. Lengthening the moments they'd known only briefly before.

...And as he and the sweet flower of youth he supposed was his beloved Fiona lay in delecti upon the dusty floor of his stationmaster's office, Gilbert Shenge recalled the times over the past twenty-five years when he had spent such nights as this in those glorious arms.

You see, Fiona loved not only gracious living but also the simple things in life; one simple thing in fact. She had also taken the trouble to invest wisely, usually upon the advice of young stockbrokers she'd seduced, the money which materialised from the multifarious ingenuity of her lover Gilbert Shenge. This was substantially the profit that the Railway never made; though both she and Shenge slept soundly with the clear consciences of those who knew that the Company books were never so much as a penny out.

Apart from expenses like paying for holidays together, odd weeks spent twice a year in small unknown resorts all over Europe or on the lovely Isle of Skye, near to the sheep, during the war, they spent little of the fortune she had been able to amass on his behalf. Shenge knew that he had Fiona to thank for that fortune now; a fortune that now, in the golden evening of their years, they would spend together. He was retired and it was all planned.

After Fiona's agreed last fling with her younger man, that morning whilst he was being presented with his inaccurate watch and parsimonious pension by that senile old pickled liver Sir George, they would be married, amid a blaze of 'News of the World' publicity, by a well known Bishop that Lady Fiona was most anxious to get even with. And then would emigrate to a mountain lodge in that part of Norway they both loved so much.

Alas as he lay in the glorious arms of the devious Mandy, he did not know, nor could he know, that his dreams and plans were not to be, but nevertheless he would soon be joining his beloved Fiona, but sadly not in Norway!

So in the morning, when Shenge awakened from the slumbers which inevitably followed his moments of passion, he found it was not with Fiona with whom he had so idly passed the night. He found too that neither he nor Mandy really seemed to care. And in that moment as the golden morning sun rose over the simmering engine shed he asked the willing creature to form the union which would prove, even to the Colonel, that Gilbert Shenge was not a 'ginger beer' nor indeed anything like that stationmaster in Jodhpur, but rather that he was fully capable of living in married harmony and bliss for the rest of his life.

For a few moments Gilbert wondered why it was the Fiona had not come but was rather relieved she hadn't.

Now Harry Trumps, who had been evicted from his lodgings only the week before for singing loudly and tunelessly in his sleep and wearing his coal-heaving boots in bed, being forced by these reduced circumstances to sleep in the station lamp room, had witnessed all that had transpired during that long night of lust. Though Trumps could not hear, he had excellent eyes…

Excellent eyes indeed. On clear nights he had often watched that young woman at number fifty-two and that was nearly a quarter of a mile away. Also he had not worked all those years without realising a thing or two about what was going on both within the running of the railway and without.

Harry Trumps also had a very useful hobby. He was a keen and highly competent photographer and his proudest possession was an 'Ensign 620' camera purchased with 'Kensitas' coupons he'd filched from the stations waste paper bins. Since Trumps did not smoke, it had taken him almost three years of constant vigilance to get it, but now Harry was determined to make that camera work for him. You see, Harry with a camera was a natural. He was one of those very rare individuals who could use the device as a natural extension of eyes, memory and imagination. Trumps had superb eyes, a thoroughly corrupt and devious memory, and probably the filthiest imagination in the world. Harry Trumps also had an extremely prying nature.

Every single event of that long night was carefully, faithfully and perfectly recorded despite Trumps having to change films four times in the half-light.

Harry Trumps also had one other gift. He knew precisely who Mandy's father was; he ought to, since he'd got the same father himself. A father he was most anxious to get even with unless, that is, he could be diverted in some way.

It would seem to the most casual observer that both brother and sister shared a common modus operandi. It must have been a family trait, which was odd since though they shared the same father, their mothers were different!

Linesend

Well, as with the passing of all great people, life soon returned to normal. And so after the death of Lady Fiona and the retirement of Gilbert Shenge, life on and around the line soon returned to normal too.

Sir George, Sleet-Ashe, Philpots and the Colonel all managed to enjoy their good fortune; most of their fortunes it is true ended up being enjoyed in the bar of the 'Flax Weaver and Pheasant' public house.

Sybil Craxton and Sebastian Wigby-Dolt were married by a certain well-known clergyman whom everybody suspected they had seen somewhere else sometime in the past, and Mandy and Gilbert Shenge were wed by special licence the very next day; before he could change his mind or the postman had delivered his letters.

Mandy and Gilbert had made their vows to each other; she promising to love him for as long as he lived and wondering where she could get hold of some 'Brasso' and he wondering how long it would be before Fiona found out.

Later that afternoon the postman called with Shenge's copy of the will and by evening Mandy was no longer in any need of any 'Brasso'.

The coroner was unable to determine exactly what it was that killed poor old Gilbert; whether it had been the shock of Lady Fiona's sudden demise, the excitement of being a millionaire or sheer exhaustion brought on by the nuptial company of the delicious Mandy and the ticking of his presentation watch.

What they did find however was an un-cashed postal-order for one pound seventeen and five pence and a will leaving all his worldly goods to his beloved Mandy. A will fortuitously dated the very afternoon of his death, witnessed by two people whom no-one in the district had ever heard of and written in a hand-writing that bore absolutely no resemblance to the stationmaster's meticulous copperplate, examples of which were to be found in the station's ledgers and the 'Transport Museum at Clapham'.

Still, all were agreed that Mandy was his legally wedded wife, and so it was that the estimable young lady became a very rich widow indeed.

It was about three weeks afterwards that Harry Trumps, proudly clutching a sheaf of black and white photographs that had arrived for him at the chemist's that very morning, and two brown packets addressed to the editor of the 'News of the World' and the Bishop of Bognor Regis respectively, knocked loudly upon the Widow Mandy's cottage door…